BIJOU ALLEY

finding
APRIL EMERY

Bijou Alley InkPress

ISBN: 979-8-9997642-0-1

For permissions, contact BijouAlleyOfficial@gmail.com

Illustration Credit: Anthony Cox

Photography Credit: Alex Richter

First Edition: August 2025

dedications

I would like to graciously thank the beta readers who not only supported me on this journey but also provided valuable feedback that contributed to the best version of the story. Breana Jobin, Danielle Hill, Brandi Deene, Kristina O'Brien, Emma Hesterman, Alessia Hughes, Paige Henry, Quinn Kirby, Tyler Jobin, Tiffany Souza, Nicole Starecheski, Carl Pace, and Melissa Edwards. I want to shine an extra light on Ian MacDonald, who was not just a beta reader but the person who cultivated and encouraged my love for writing.

This book would be a jumbled mess without my talented editor, Molly Logue, who pushed me to be a better writer, develop stronger storylines, and made me laugh along the way.

I want to recognize my mom, Terry, and my dad, Dennis, who have supported my love of storytelling from the very beginning.

Lastly, I'd like to thank Anthony, Charlie, and Fletcher, who unconditionally cheered me on as I typed away at the computer for hours at a time.

This book has been stuck in my mind for the last ten years, and now, I'm thrilled it can be in yours.

table of contents

finding

APRIL EMERY

good evening, Riley

A gleeful squeal erupted throughout the room as April rolled a ball down her colorful slide. Riley was amazed at how the simplest of toys could enrapture her favorite toddler.

"Go April! Go April!" Riley sang as she clapped to emphasize April's accomplishment. April mirrored her actions with her newly tooth-filled grin.

Thunder evolved from a slight shudder to a noticeable roar, overpowering the sweet tunes emanating from April's toy. April jumped as the shingles on the roof rattled, and the windows whistled as the wind passed. Branches from neighboring trees brushed against the siding of Riley's home as the clouds rushed overhead. Confused by the noises, Riley did her best to comfort her.

"No worries, April. Just a bit of thunder. Rain is good for the plants, remember?"

April stared blankly at her, blinking only once before continuing to mash her blocks against the carpet. Riley rose to her knees to peek over her velvet green couch to read the time. 7:47 blinked on the microwave.

April's mother, Kendra, mentioned that her husband, Quincy, would be picking their daughter up around 8 PM.

Kendra described that he drove a white Buick and that he should be eager to meet her. Riley had been April's nanny for nearly four months and had never met Quincy.

Though a seemingly mysterious fellow, April's father seemed to be well-loved by the community. Before Riley became involved with their family, she used to read article after article about his acts of service with law enforcement. During his work as a pharmacist, he created one of the first Drug Monitoring Programs in Chicago, significantly impacting the ongoing crisis.

Kendra told Riley that he frequently traveled for work, leaving her to care for their daughter on her own. All Riley had of April's father were the pictures plastered on the walls of the family's home. Kendra's love for April was infectious through their interactions, but even without meeting her father, you could tell by the way he looked at April that she was his everything.

Riley joining their lives felt serendipitous. It allowed Kendra to take much-needed time for herself. Riley and April had been inseparable since they met. Watching her a few times a month quickly turned into a few times a week once Kendra observed their chemistry.

Riley began the daunting task of scooping up the strewn-about toys April had chosen to play with for the evening. She repeatedly threw them toward the mountainous toy bin in the corner of her living room. April had since abandoned her slide and tried gathering the rest of the balls with Riley.

"Great job!" Riley said, running her hand through April's dark, ringlet curly hair. As April tidied, Riley noticed her stance start to crumble; her steps wobbled.

"Getting sleepy, April?"

"Night night," April yawned, falling back on her bottom and staring off into the distance.

"Your dad will be here soon," Riley whispered.

"Daddy?" April questioned, almost puzzled, like she wasn't expecting him to be home. April flopped on her belly, butt in the air, and began to suck her thumb.

Riley dimmed the lights, pulled April's favorite blanket from the couch, and draped it over her back. She rubbed in a circular motion until April's breathing began to slow, and her eyes drifted shut. Thankfully, it didn't take long; it never did. The pattern of their nighttime routine felt rhythmic and effortless.

During the brief stillness of the evening, Riley softly puttered around her living room, cleaning up remaining toys and reassembling April's diaper bag. Reaching into her pocket, she grabbed her phone and waited for the screen to illuminate. A black screen reflected her puzzled face like a mirror. "Dead, like always." She muttered, rolling her eyes as she walked back to her bedroom to plug it in.

The phone rested on her nightstand as she tiptoed back into the living room, hoping April was still zonked. With a sigh of relief, as she gazed at the sleeping girl, she took this golden opportunity to grab a quick snack from the kitchen. April may have been relatively easy to look after, but constantly singing, dancing, and playing definitely worked up an appetite.

Another thunderclap radiated through the room, making the chandelier light flicker once, then twice. Peeking through the kitchen window, Riley gaped at the storm thrashing against the pane. The racing droplets began to glow fluorescently as a car raced up the driveway.

"*8:02. That must be Quincy*," Riley thought. She peeked around the corner to see April now sprawled out on her back, gripping her blanket. Her tiny thumb barely hung out of her drool-covered mouth.

"*Too easy*." Riley walked back into the living room and carefully slipped April's rainbow shoes on her tiny toes.

The rain pounded relentlessly against the roof of Riley's home. She wrapped April in a blanket and draped her over her shoulder, feeling the toddler's head nestle perfectly into her neck. A flash of blinding light beamed through every window. Riley anticipated the deafening thunder to follow that would undoubtedly wake April. Surprisingly, she dozed completely unbothered. Riley plunked down on the couch with April to await Quincy's arrival at her doorstep. She felt herself drifting off, the comforting weight and warmth of April enveloping her.

Riley felt like she'd only blinked before she was startled awake by an obnoxious honk from outside.

"Uhh…" Riley grumbled as April slept calmly on her chest. The time was twelve past eight. Riley gently rose from the couch.

"*I guess he's not coming inside,*" she quietly thought, irritated by Quincy's rudeness. She shrugged off her opinion and slipped on a pair of canvas shoes that were a size too big, hurled the diaper bag over her unoccupied shoulder, and began the trek to Quincy's car in the pouring rain.

Riley had hoped Quincy would meet them at the door and chat for a while, so she could rave about how much she loved his daughter (and so they wouldn't have to stand in blistering winds and pouring rain). But instead, Riley's front door blasted open to reveal an empty front porch. The headlights of the white Buick glowed in the distance. April muttered something in her sleep as the raindrops melted into her caramel skin.

Riley's feet squelched with each step through the grass as she avoided deep puddles. She held the diaper bag over April's head in a feeble attempt to keep her dry.

Finally approaching the car, Riley reached for the silver handle of the backseat, but it wouldn't budge. After a few seconds, she heard it click and tried to open the door as smoothly as possible, fighting the wind to not jostle April awake. As she opened the door, Riley saw that the car was sparkling clean, much to her surprise. April was notorious for leaving cereal o's and empty juice boxes all over Riley's backseat. Mild jealousy formed, being able to see the floor not covered in stains and toys.

A rush of floral aroma invaded her nose as she noticed the clips in the vents. Raindrops flooded the cracks between the car and the doorframe and sporadically splashed onto the backseat's floor mats.

Drenched and cold, Riley shivered as she carefully placed April in the pristine, bright pink car seat. It looked like it just came out of the box.

"Hi Quincy, nice to meet you," Riley squeaked out in a hushed but excited tone. The man in the front seat was swallowed up by a light gray hoodie peppered with raindrops. The night sky shadowed a red embroidered emblem on his sleeve. The man's posture seemed stark, his hands firm on the wheel at ten and two. He turned ever-so-slightly to greet Riley, and the overhead light created deeper shadows on his already-darkened face.

"Good evening, Riley," he retorted, his voice deep but soft. Riley tossed the diaper bag over April onto the seat next to her and secured the last buckle on her seatbelt. As it clicked, April snapped awake as if she were having a bad dream, and began screaming.

"Oh, no, April! What's wrong? Everything is alright," Riley reassured the squirming girl.

"NO! RY RY!" April screamed. Riley rubbed her head and held her flailing hands, trying her best to soothe her back to sleep.

"*It must just be the storm,*" Riley thought. Riley gave her a quick hug. April clung to her shirt with an intense grip. Riley tried her best to release her hands, watching as tears welled in April's green eyes, begging for Riley to stay. Riley looked up to Quincy for reassurance or input on the situation, but with both hands still gripping the wheel, he continued to look straight forward. He softly grunted with frustration.

"I'm sure you've had a long day," Riley sighed apologetically. "She's not usually like this." She was met with only silence from the man in the front seat. "I'll see you next week, April!" Riley cheerfully assured her as she finally loosened April's grip from her shirt and closed the car door.

Before Riley could even step back from the car, it shifted gears and sped in reverse down the driveway, right over Riley's left shoe. She was stunned. Had her shoes been the right size, her toes would've been crushed. *"Why was he in such a hurry?"*

Standing speechless in the pouring rain, she pondered as she watched the car exit her driveway, hop the curb, and squeal onto the street below. She watched in disbelief as the bright red taillights slowly trailed out of sight. *"Everyone has their off days, I guess."*

Riley shuffled along her front yard, sinking into the lawn with each step. She kicked her feet against the stoop, gawking at the tire mark on top of her shoe. She trudged inside her house and locked the deadbolt behind her. A soaking wet Riley sank back onto the door with a huff before peeling off her waterlogged socks. She closed her eyes and felt a familiar warmth brush against her legs. Looking down, she saw her trusty companion, Griddle - a half-blind black and orange Persian cat. He was the jealous type and would always hide when Riley had April over. He only ever came back out when she was gone.

"You have me all to yourself again, buddy," Riley cooed, stroking Griddle's back. The time was now 8:22 PM. Riley left a trail of drips as she walked through her home into the bedroom. Griddle wasn't far behind. The rest of Saturday night was still ahead of her. Riley smiled in excitement at the idea of the evening filled with her favorite shows, her favorite snacks, and her favorite cat lying on her lap to warm her up after being soaked in the storm. After checking the radar, it seemed the worst of said storm was over.

Now wrapped in her coziest pajamas, fuzzy robe, and slippers, she danced down the hallway into the kitchen. The crinkle of plastic tearing from a bag of microwave popcorn sounded like her own personal symphony. Setting the timer for two minutes, Riley leaned back against her cabinets. She watched the microwave light bounce as she anticipated her warm, salty snack. The drone of the microwave was hypnotic, and she zoned out, recounting April's drop-off.

Something just felt…different. Off. Kendra was always so kind, engaging, and thorough when it came to anything regarding April. Quincy was…inattentive. Preoccupied, maybe?

"*Maybe I'm overthinking this,*" Riley thought, buzzing sounds swirling in her head. "But he *ran over* my *foot*!" She said, exasperated and in disbelief at the fact that someone could be in such a hur-

beep...beep...beep

Riley snapped back to reality with the smell of warm butter and salt wafting through the air, pausing only for a moment before shaking the steam from the crinkly brown bag and walking to the couch.

She turned on her show, threw Griddle's favorite blanket on top of her legs, and hoped that her furry friend could take her mind off of the strange encounter with Quincy.

The show only acted as background noise to Riley's racing thoughts. She had a sinking feeling that she just couldn't shake. She reached for a handful of popcorn as her doorbell rang. It made her jump so hard that popcorn rained down onto the floor. Griddle, who was slowly making his way onto Riley's lap, bolted down the hall into the bedroom. Her sudden startle turned into stone-still shock, as she wasn't expecting anyone else for the night. Riley tossed the blanket off of her lap and crept towards the front door, grabbing an umbrella from the coat rack for…protection?

"When you live alone, anything is better than nothing," she reasoned, accidentally stepping into the puddles of water she left earlier. As she peeked through the front door window, she was happily surprised by a familiar face - Kendra. Riley's tension melted into relief as she exhaled.

"I can't wait to talk to her about how weird Quincy was." She happily opened the door. Kendra stood on the porch, hair glistening with stray raindrops from the passing storm.

"Hey Riley," Kendra beamed, always in an uplifting mood.

"Hi Kendra! I didn't know you'd be coming by tonight. Come in!" Riley said, swinging the door open wider so Kendra could step inside.

"I won't stay long. Sorry that I didn't message you sooner." Riley patted her pockets and realized her phone was still on the charger.

Kendra combed down her frizzy hair with her hands. "Quincy called me and said that work was keeping him late again. He has asked that I grab April from you tonight. I know I told you he'd be here around eight. Of course, we're more than happy to pay you for the extra time."

As if Riley's skin wasn't already ghostly pale, she turned nearly translucent as her blood ran cold. Kendra's words became an echo, replaying like a broken record. Riley couldn't move, not even to blink.

"Riley?" Kendra questioned. "Are you feeling okay?" As Kendra watched her demeanor shift, Riley couldn't hear a thing. Her stomach dropped as if she'd driven down a steep hill, and then off a cliff. The memories of the evening played over and over and over again in her head at warp speed until her knees buckled, and she fell to the floor.

"RILEY!" Kendra screamed, grabbing her shoulders. "What's going on?" The room began to spin as the colors of the paintings on the walls melded with the houseplants hanging from the window frames. Everything swirled together until the room turned black.

Kendra's muffled screams made it feel like Riley was underwater. She felt the thumps of Kendra's footsteps, frantically running throughout the house in search of her daughter, April. Where was April?

———

Bright, white lights awakened Riley. An intense buzzing noise from overhead had become far too familiar. The same recurring dream continued to haunt her. There was no escape.

This nightmare wasn't just a bad dream, though - it was an unfortunate reality. Riley sat up and hung her legs over the bed, as she did every morning. She wiped the sleep away from her eyes, trying her best to adjust to the brightness. She slid into her complimentary slippers, barely thicker than a piece of paper. She stood from the bed and walked to the mirror, hardly clean enough to see her reflection. Next to her mirror was a small, dingy calendar, tattered and torn. Watching the days fade away made Riley less hopeful and more anxious.

It had been two weeks. Two weeks since Riley's encounter with Qui... The Man In Gray. It had been two weeks since she had seen April. Just one and a half weeks since she was officially arrested and thrown into Clarendon Correctional Center to await the next steps.

The days after April's disappearance were a hazy blur, filled with questions, doubt, and speculation. Kendra's incriminating recap of the incident, Quincy's prior relationship with law enforcement, and Riley's inability to speak coherently created the perfect storm of suspicion. That was enough for Riley to be taken into custody as the only suspect. Her fate was now in the hands of a judge and jury, who were eagerly waiting to decide her fate.

A blaring chime bounced off the walls of her cell, indicating a new day was about to start.

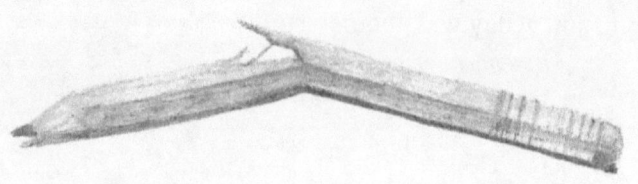

the news knows all

Riley didn't remember the last time she slept normally. The mattress in her cell was thin, lumpy, and itchy. Sandpaper-like fibers poked her skin each night. But the pain she felt from the scratches was nothing compared to the pain in her head.

The events from that night consumed her every thought. Retracing each step and detail, down to the colors of the balls April rolled down her slide. Riley remembered everything, which made her body twitch with anger. If she could recount every detail, why couldn't she pinpoint what went wrong? The man she saw in the car perfectly fits Kendra's description of Quincy. Even with the shadows from the car light and the flashes of lightning blurring his facial features. How did The Man In Gray have the same car, the same pick-up time, and Riley's address? Even with every detail, nothing made sense to her.

She walked silently. The metal clinking of opening cell doors bounced around the concrete hall and pierced her eardrums.

Neighboring inmates were jeering and shouting toward her direction. All Riley could do was shuffle along the filthy, scuffed floor, staring at each footstep colliding with the tile. She rounded the corner and arrived at the dining hall. The officer motioned for her to get in line and grab her tray.

"Thank you," Riley said to the guard as he turned back to usher more inmates.

The guard looked back confused. For a moment, Riley forgot where she was. Simple manners were always a standard in her behavior, though here, they seemed foreign and inappropriate. Riley still didn't fully understand the culture within the jail. Nobody was kind. Nobody made conversation. Everything felt cold and sterile.

She avoided eye contact as she shuffled her way down the breakfast line. A four-ounce box of orange juice concentrate was slammed onto her tray. Stale cereal o's were poured into a bowl by an inmate working their morning shift, followed by a splash of skim milk.

Another inmate spooned a ladle of canned fruit cocktail into the open section of her tray. The juices splashed onto the side and trickled underneath. The last inmate laid down a piece of toast - the end of the loaf - with a small slab of semi-melted butter. Riley used to thank them too, but was met with snarls and eyerolls early on. "Another goodie-goodie," they sneered, accompanied by bullying laughter. This time, she simply grabbed her tray and slowly walked to an empty table.

Riley examined the miserable meal in front of her. She figured the safest place to start was her cereal. She reminisced about the breakfasts she used to cook at home. Breakfast was always Riley's favorite meal. Crispy bacon, cheesy eggs, pillowy pancakes drowning in syrup and whipped cream. Her daydream was interrupted by whispers around the dining hall and the feeling of heat pointed in her direction. After coming back to reality, Riley looked around the room to see nearly every inmate staring at her.

"*What did I do now*?" she thought, trying not to give them any attention while nervously shoveling another spoonful of cereal into her mouth.

"Some story, huh?" An inmate shouted across the room.

The nearest guard slapped their hand on the table, which startled the inmate enough to turn back around. Just then, the small 19-inch television in the corner of the room caught Riley's gaze, causing her spoon to drop.

"*UNFORTUNATE NEWS THIS MORNING.*"

The news anchor stated bluntly.

"*STILL NO SIGN OF APRIL EMERY FELLOWES, THE MISSING TODDLER FROM CLARENDON HILLS. RILEY MICHAELS, WHOSE BAIL IS CURRENTLY SET AT FIFTEEN THOUSAND DOLLARS, WAS THE LAST PERSON TO HAVE SEEN APRIL AND IS THE ONLY SUSPECT. AT THIS TIME,*

MICHAELS WILL REMAIN IN CUSTODY UNTIL FURTHER QUESTIONING AT CLARENDON CORRECTIONAL CENTER THIS AFTERNOON."

Riley's eyes pulsed and locked to the floor. The heat from the inmates' menacing eyes only fueled the fire in the pit of her stomach. They all knew about April. They all knew about *her*. This was the worst thing to ever happen in their small town, and the media was eating it up. From the comments made within the halls and common areas, the inmates didn't seem to be on Riley's side. They were extremely accusatory, demanding she give up the details of where April was, "or else." Riley, too in shock to verbalize what truly happened that night, dealt with the wrath of the inmates instead of giving them what they shouted at her for. Bruises riddled her body from passing punches. Riley couldn't believe this was her new home. Then, the anchor's voice rang through the room again.

"IF ANYONE HAS CLUES TO FELLOWES' WHEREABOUTS, WE URGE YOU TO COME FORWARD AND CONTACT THE LOCAL AUTHORITIES. NOW, OUR NEXT STORY THIS EVENING..."

She wasn't frozen by the fact that she was named the sole suspect in the case - she was numb hearing that April *still hadn't been found*. It had been 14 days without April begging for animal crackers, spinning in circles until she fell, or drooling through her bibs because she had a new tooth coming in. Was she safe? Was she scared? Riley felt her hands tremble as stale cereal crept back up her throat.

"Wait," she whispered out loud, swallowing hard as she recounted the broadcast.

Riley's eyes scanned her tray, trying to understand the announcer's words.

"*UNTIL FURTHER QUESTIONING THIS AFTERNOON.*"

"Questioning? What questioning?" She whispered, hoping the answer would surface.

When she was booked on the night of the incident, Riley struggled to even say her own name. Fear, anger, and confusion tangled together into a trap that caught her words in her throat. The interrogation that followed was short and useless. How could they get the answers they wanted when Riley didn't have them? She wondered when they would come back to her. When would they give another chance to tell her side of the story? When could she start searching for April?

It was shocking to learn from the news that today was the day all those questions could be answered. Riley tried her best to collect her thoughts and compose herself in preparation—she wanted to be ready, and this time, she was going to be cooperative.

———

The first couple of days in jail were unsettling. They threw Riley in a dingy, isolated cell. The only thing that kept her company was the ghosts of former inmates, living in the scratches and tally marks on the walls. Riley knew she needed something to keep her mind off her fate, so she inquired about a job. The guards didn't seem thrilled to grant her request, but said they would check back with her if a position was available. She doubted they ever would.

After her rather eventful breakfast ended, Riley was surprised as she was released to go to the work program desk. Before April was in the picture, Riley was a children's book author. Ever since she was a kid, she loved to write and illustrate the wildest stories. Her big imagination lived on every scrap of paper she found in her house, a mosaic of wild adventures and the pictures that brought them to life.

Her mother helped stoke the fire of her inner world by playing a game with her - they'd give each other a word, and from that one word, they'd have to build an entire story. It was Riley's favorite activity, and each word was a stone brick in the biggest, tallest castle of her life, where she and her mom ruled the world. Looking back at it now, it was just a silly game they played to pass the time, but to Riley, it was the spark that lit a blazing love she carried for storytelling. She continued her passion through high school and college, pursuing English and journalism, and graduating with a bachelor's in communications. Her love for writing went hand in hand with learning.

She decided that after this summer with April, she wanted to enroll back in school to get her master's. Maybe she'd even get her doctorate. Her big, tall castle felt so far away now; her flame faded to a single ember in the brutalist architecture of the jail.

Riley walked up to the work program desk. The guard took one look at Riley before saying,

"You must be Michaels. It's your lucky day. Our English teacher just got sentenced and transferred. Looks like you'll fit in nicely based on your education." The rock Riley swallowed in her throat blossomed into butterflies in her stomach. She cracked a side smile and nodded at the guard.

"Don't get too excited," the guard snarked, scribbling signatures on papers. "You're not getting paid for this. Inmates must be here for at least six months before receiving compensation."

"Anything to keep my mind busy is compensation enough," Riley said under her breath. He paused for a moment, squinting disdainfully at her, before signing the last piece of paper to give to her.

"This explains what your expectations are within this program. Read it. Sign it." He said sternly.

Riley quickly scanned the document. The tapping of the guards' fingers on the desk distracted her. From what she gathered, Clarendon Correctional Center (Triple C, as the inmates call it) would allow detainees to obtain their G.E.D. while awaiting their sentencing in hopes of giving them a better chance at life when they were released.

Riley's heart fluttered at the idea of helping someone make use of their time here, and English was something she knew like the back of her hand. She signed the paper, and the guard called for a colleague on his walkie-talkie.

"Roger." A female voice called. A few moments later, a voice echoed from down the hallway.

"C'mon, Michaels," the tall, blonde woman said. She wore her hair in a tight, slick-back bun, like she had been in the military.

Riley marched down the hall, where the guard encouraged her to walk in front of her through a set of double doors. The guard was eerily close behind Riley, making the hair on the back of her neck raise as they approached the room.

"Aren't you the girl they're all talking about on TV?" The woman questioned. Riley turned back.

"Yes," she said hesitantly, hoping this wouldn't result in another beating. They quickly approached a dead end with a big metal door. The guard shoved Riley aside as she unlinked the keys from her belt to unlock the door.

"Hmm," she said, fiddling with her keys to find the right one. "That's some story. I hope they find the girl. Two weeks is a long time to be missing."

Riley was astounded and enraged at the guard's statement. What an insult, as if Riley hadn't counted every second she'd been away from April. Her blood rose from a simmer to a boil, but she did her best to stay calm and quiet. She was no stranger to retaliation, but she didn't want to meet it again - not right now. After what felt like hours, the door finally unlocked and opened.

The guard flicked the light switch to reveal a shell of a classroom with three rows of school chairs and desks - each riddled with cracks, dents, and etched doodles from countless frustrated students. Dull light filtered through the grimy windows, painting the room in various shades of gray. The front of the room had a single desk that was slightly larger than the others and a whiteboard that was stained with markers from previous lessons. Riley sighed deeply. "*I can work with this,*" she thought to herself, still maintaining her optimism.

"Sit at the desk and wait for the others," the guard barked, pushing her to the front of the room.

Riley nearly tripped over her own feet, scrambling to catch herself from the surprise force. The guard scoffed, leaning up against the wall near the door.

"You know, they have a pretty hard time keeping this position filled. Most inmates can't handle the torment from the others," the guard said. "Are you an English teacher or just looking for something to do?"

Riley paused for a moment before responding. The guard's tone made her feel lower than dirt, but shockingly, she felt somewhat comforted by someone, *anyone,* talking to her without bringing up April.

"Not quite," Riley replied, kicking her legs back and forth as she sat in the squeaky desk chair. "I have a degree in communications, and I'm an author."

"Whoooaaa, we've got ourselves a celebrity at Triple C," the guard taunted.

Riley sunk, a rare meaningful conversation quickly souring. The room fell to stagnation, except for the lights buzzing above her head and the wind sneaking through a crack in the window.

She closed her eyes for only a moment before the door swung open, and in came seven inmates. Scowls covered their faces. The guard showed them to their desks and promptly left without saying a word. The room was silent again - all eyes were on Riley. Her eyes widened, and she looked at the blonde guard, who was fiddling with her uniform. She looked up and rolled her eyes.

"Well, go ahead, teach something."

Riley's stomach dropped as the inmates at their desks were getting impatient.

"Are there any materials or books? Lesson plans, maybe?" Riley questioned, standing up from her desk.

"Mmmm, I don't know," the guard said, unbothered, turning to the other inmates. "What do you guys usually do in here?"

One inmate piped up. "We don't do much of anything. The teacher would read us a textbook and ask us to write about what we read. That's about it".

Riley looked around the seemingly empty room until her eyes locked on a small filing cabinet covered in dust in the corner. She turned back to the guard, motioning if it was okay to investigate. The guard nodded, and Riley shuffled over. After jiggling the handle for what felt like minutes, the creaky cabinet door opened to reveal a few pencils, tattered sheets of lined paper, and a few English 101 textbooks with broken spines and ripped pages. Riley had to think of something fast.

"Anytime now, Michaels," the guard called from across the room with her arms crossed.

Riley grabbed everything she could from the cabinet and walked back to her desk. She opened the textbook to see that most of the pages had been scribbled on by former inmates.

"Screw this," one comment wrote.

"School is for chumbs." Although Riley was convinced they meant "chumps", the irony made her chuckle. She slapped the book closed and decided to go off the cuff.

She walked over to each inmate and handed them a pencil and a piece of paper. The first inmate was large, muscular, and stiff-

24

looking. Her dark brunette hair was slick with grease, and her deep brown eyes never unlocked from intensely staring at Riley. She was analyzing her every move. She immediately snapped her pencil in half and threw it on the floor in front of Riley's feet like a toddler. The officer quickly piped up.

"Hey Syke. This is a voluntary program. You're more than welcome to spend this time cleaning the bottom of my shoe if that will make you feel more fulfilled," the guard warned.

Syke clicked her tongue and picked the pencil up off the floor, giving a big huff in the process.

"Okay…" Riley timidly said after passing out the rest of the materials. "I'm not sure what you've learned up until this point, but we're going to do what I think is a fun activity." Riley beamed, excited to share one of her favorite writing prompts. She was met with straight faces, lacking any and all emotion. Her smile quickly faded into a dejected smirk.

"I want you all to write about the dream you had last night." The inmates all looked at each other for a moment before one spoke up.

"What's that have to do with me gettin' my G.E.D. princess?" She said, puzzled and slightly annoyed.

"Well," Riley said, as she gripped her toes in her shoes and shifted her body weight from side to side. Her fingernails grazed the inside of her palms.

"The more you do something, the better you become at it. And writing is a huge part of your G.E.D. test."

"What if I don't fucking remember my dream, hm?" Syke quickly chimed in, mocking Riley.

"Yeah," another said in agreement.

"I get it. I have nights where I don't remember my dreams either. Uh, write about a dream that you have for yourself. Maybe what you see yourself doing when you get out of here. Then we can analyze your writing as a group." Riley suggested.

Moans and groans filled the room after listening to her assignment. The guard loudly cleared her throat and held up the bottom of her shoe to send a message. The grunting stopped, and all of the inmates began to write.

The sounds of graphite scraping across the lined paper was oddly soothing to Riley. She stared down at her own blank paper. Her mind trembled thinking about the terrifying women in front of her. The pencil began to slip from her grip as her palms oozed sweat. Reaching for the paper, her fingers grazed over a crack in the desk. Its roughness emulated the jagged edge of her dwindling hope.

She looked up and watched the clock on the wall. With each ticking second, Riley felt a panic attack start as the darkness began to engulf her thoughts. "No," she whispered to herself. "*We're past this.*" Riley picked up the pencil and let her mind flow out through her fingers.

26

She feverishly wrote about the only thing that would bring her peace, April. Memories of how the ringlets of April's curls used to get caught in Riley's fingers. She wrote about how her green eyes sparkled and nearly matched the color of the grass surrounding the park they frequented. How the drool illuminating her cheeks never seemed to end, especially after cutting a tooth.

She wrote about how strong her relationship with Kendra had gotten. How she acted not only as a friend, but a mother figure who filled the void in Riley's life. She wrote about how when she came down with the flu a few months ago, Kendra showed up unannounced, holding an electric blanket and a fresh pot of homemade chicken and rice soup. Riley was certain the broth was what cleared her illness. She noted the time that Kendra held her weeping body on the floor of her living room, and stroked her straggly, strawberry hair as she sulked about her failed manuscripts. Kendra's encouraging words rang in her ears to this day and pushed her to continue her dream. Something she was inches away from giving up on.

As she wrote, she forgot all about the inmates in front of her. For a moment, she was back home in her office, in her emerald green chair, with Griddle curled up on her lap, looking out over her backyard. She watched as the sunlight filtered through the leaves and made patterns on the ground. Her coffee's sweet vanilla aroma filled the room as she completely lost herself in her writing. Her mind felt fully at peace for the first time in two weeks. Life was normal again.

Riley's trance was brutally interrupted by the faint noises of someone calling her name and the sound of her pencil tip snapping, stopping her sentence dead in its tracks. She looked up to check on the inmates and was startled by two new guards standing over her.

"Michaels, are you deaf?" One of them directs at her, slamming his hand on the table.

Riley was stunned. What did she miss?

"We need to cut your class short." The other guard said as they came around the desk and grabbed Riley's arm. All of the inmates put their pencils down to eavesdrop. Surely, they were thrilled there was something else to do than write about their hopes and dreams. Disoriented from her daydream, Riley hesitantly left the classroom and followed the guards into the hallway.

"I look forward to hearing about your dreams when I get back," Riley yelped over her shoulder.

A roar of laughter led by Syke echoed as the door slammed behind her.

"Heh," the guard chuckled. "You might not be coming back, Michaels."

Syke - 0

Shadows gnawed at the hallway's edges as Riley hesitantly took each step. A guard stood on both sides of her as if they were protecting their surroundings from a convicted murderer or a clinical psycho. The guard on the left grabbed her arm and pulled her through a large metal door, where she was met with a flash of bright white light.

The room was no larger than the quaint reading nook tucked in the spare bedroom of Riley's home. Though unlike her nook, this space felt claustrophobic instead of inviting. The walls were poorly patched with plaster in an attempt to cover the fist-sized holes that met her eye level. A galvanized metal chair with a crack in the center sat in front of a steel table. A warm lamp illuminated the room.

"Sit," the left guard demanded.

Riley slinked to the middle of the room. Before fully sitting, the guard cuffed her ankle to the leg of the chair and walked out of the room without another word. In front of her, she saw a framed windowpane with glass that resembled TV static. Behind the glass were three faint silhouettes, two standing and one sitting.

Her eyes snapped closed as she inhaled deeply, focusing on normalizing her irregular breathing. The smell of stale, musty mop water filled her nostrils. Her pulse radiated in her temples and down the side of her neck. Sweat from her palms dripped onto the table below her.

The door swung open, slamming into the wall behind it. Riley consciously kept her eyes closed.

"Riley? Riley Michaels?" A woman's soft voice questioned. Riley exhaled and opened her eyes to reveal a short, frail woman with wire glasses and a friendly smile. She was wearing a floral pink dress that swished at the bottom when she closed the door with elegance. The woman laid a mountain of papers, sticky notes, and folders on the table, labeled with her name in all caps, which made Riley's eyes burn.

"I'm Detective Cho," she said, placing a warm, comforting hand on top of Riley's.

"I'm here to talk about the events within your case and help get you out of here. Hopefully, I can set your mind at ease." She chuckled. "And just so you know, this is not an interrogation. I just want to ask you a few questions. In fact, let's get these cuffs off your leg. I think you've been through enough in these last few weeks, haven't you?" The detective's brow wrinkled with seemingly genuine concern. Riley couldn't help but let out a subtle "yes."

The detective pulled a key from her back pocket and unlinked the chains from the table.

Riley eyed Ms. Cho up and down, observing every divot on her lips that encased her toothy smile. This sweet, older woman beamed with a glowing yellow aura. She resembled a puzzle piece that ended up in the wrong box. Though trustworthy by optics, something deep within Riley's gut twisted with concern. Unsure if this was a test, she sat motionless in her seat. Cho's smile faded as her eyebrows raised.

"Go on now, sweetie," Cho said reassuringly. "Get up, walk around a bit."

Riley dismissed her instincts and took the opportunity to release her nervous energy. Short strolls and leg shakes always helped clear her mind. She scooted the metal chair back, scraping the bottom of the legs across the floor, filling the air with a high-pitched sound. After pacing for a moment, Riley stopped to look at Cho.

"Okay," she said confidently. "I'm ready to talk."

Riley relayed every detail of the night April disappeared, down to the purple sparkly socks that encased her tiny toes. She described the shadows that caressed The Man In Gray's face in the front seat of his car.

The absolute panic in Kendra's voice as she ransacked Riley's home looking for her daughter. The red and blue fluorescent lights that illuminated every window of her home as she was carried out in handcuffs, unable to stand on her own. The questions, endless questions that she didn't have the answers to at the time. The who, what, when, where, and why. The shame, defeat, disgust, and terror she felt as she was thrown into a cold cell as that unforgettable night drew to a close.

She didn't skip a beat and felt her body zing with adrenaline when she finished. Riley felt as if she had been talking for hours, and without a clock to check, she very well could have been. The edges of her lips were cracked. The words she spoke felt like sand, gritty and suffocating but liberating. She was confident that she had solidified her innocence.

A long silence lingered from the time Riley stopped speaking to when Cho started. A smirk was glued on the detective's face. Riley, trying to match her energy, gave a slight smile in hopes of receiving any type of reaction.

"Thank you for being so cooperative, Riley. The information you gave us is incredibly important for this case. I do have a few more questions, though."

Feeling a rush of ease, Riley stood tall. She braced her hands on the back of the chair and released the tension within her shoulders. "Sure. Whatever you need."

Cho feverishly flipped through her stack of papers until she found some scribbled notes, clearly written well before their meeting.

"Ah, yes," Cho said. Her eyes gleamed almost menacingly as she scanned her scribbled sentences. "You had mentioned that the man driving the…Buick, was it? Ran over your foot as he was speeding away with the girl. But when we first started chatting, you seemed to be walking around with no problem. Surely if he ran over your foot, you would have some discomfort, especially without medical attention. Wouldn't you, hmm?"

Riley stared at Cho, dumbfounded. *This,* this *was the crucial piece of information she'd unearthed from that chaotic night?*" She thought.

Warmth suddenly drained from the room, quickly replaced by the unexpected graze of distrust. Riley released her gaze from the detective to focus on the silhouettes behind the faded glass. They were distracting, shifting uncomfortably in their seats.

As the light above them flickered, Riley's unease grew. Her pores oozed with doubt. The air in the room was stale and suffocating. Feeling like the walls were inching closer toward her body, she decided that if another second passed in this unbearable silence, her head might explode from the stress.

"My…shoes were too big." Her voice diffused through the room, echoing off each wall.

"Excuse me?" Cho asked gently but condescendingly, genuinely confused.

"I grabbed the wrong shoes when I went to bring April outside. They were one size too large. Are you going to hang my innocence on a pair of shoes?" Riley sat emotionless. Apprehension and anxiety surged through her body.

"You *are* the only one living in the home, is that correct?"

"The only one walking on two legs," Riley uttered, trying to lighten the room. Cho looked up from her notes for only a moment before her pen scratched the paper again.

Riley walked to the table and sank back into her seat. The metal chair was brittle and cold on her back.

"So then, the shoes belong to?"

"Kendra. April's mother. She'd left them at my house the week before. She brought home my favorite flip-flops instead."

Memories of Kendra came flooding to the forefront of her mind. The infectious laugh that filled the room when Riley would tell a joke, even the bad ones. The spontaneous sleep-overs Riley would have at their house, and waking up to a full array of fresh breakfast foods in the morning. Kendra's unhealthy obsession with

34

shopping, even for things she didn't need, like another pair of canvas shoes.

Riley's eyes stupidly welled with tears, remembering the footwear. What a silly detail to get emotional over. A lone teardrop rolled off her cheek and splashed onto the thigh of her pants, leaving a darker spot amongst the bright orange. She quickly rubbed her hands across her blotchy cheeks, embarrassed by the sudden emotion. She didn't want to appear any more vulnerable than she'd already felt.

Still sitting in the same spot as she started, Detective Cho carefully closed her folder full of papers. "Ms. Michaels," she stated, like a parent would speak to a child. "Would you like a tissue?"

"No," Riley snapped. She slowly began understanding Cho's charming and twee facade. Nausea coiled her gut. Her cheeks, once blotchy and stained with tears, were now fuming and hot to the touch.

"Well," Cho said, standing up from the table. "I think I have everything I need for now. We greatly appreciate you taking the time to speak with me today." Her eyes narrowed, and she flashed a Cheshire cat smile.

The detective vanished through the door without a trace. The silhouettes in the window dissipated, except for one who sat stock-still like a cardboard cutout. Riley sat in the room completely alone, with only her thoughts to accompany her.

"What the hell was THAT?" Riley thought bluntly.

One of the guards busted through the door behind her. "Back to your cell, Michaels. You're dismissed from your job for the rest of the day. Let's go." The glimmer of hope that her story granted her release had been shattered.

———

Like a needle stuck in the groove of a record, Riley's thoughts spun on repeat, retracing the labyrinthian twists and turns of their earlier conversation. The dim light from the lamp above her glittered off the bed frame near her feet.

Riley craned her tense neck to see the time on the clock - 9:56 AM. Having the rest of the day ahead of her, she mustered every bit of strength in her body to get up from her cot to rinse the dried, crusted sweat from her brow. Her fingers slipped from the edge of the sink before gripping it tightly, like she would cease to exist in this moment if nothing were to anchor her. A familiar empty stare met her own in the blurred mirror.

"Is this really what I look like?"

Her eyes were drawn to her sunken jawline and blotchy skin. Two weeks felt like two years, especially after the nightmare of an interrogation she had just endured. Her head hung over the sink as she turned on the faucet. Ice-cold water ran over her fingers, turning her nails a subtle hue of purple.

It was as if every speck of hope, any feeling of warmth, drowned in the frigid stream racing down the drain. Riley was circling the drain, too, carried away in the repetitive lull of the rushing water. The hypnotic numbness shattered as two guards stopped in front of her cell.

"On the wall!" A guard bellowed.

Riley was still a novice at understanding the jail lingo, but she knew exactly what to do when she heard that order. With the water still gushing, she ran to the nearest wall. She spread her legs and placed her hands on the wall above her head.

She watched as the drips of water left her hand and highlighted the walls' cracks and imperfections. Her cell door clicked and creaked open. The vibrations of footsteps shot up through Riley's legs. "*Surely, this was just a routine search?*" She questioned silently until the guard spoke. She had been through this only once before.

"I know you've had the luxury of having this suite all to yourself, Michaels, but that changes today. Play nice."

Riley's blood ran cold as she tried to recount what the guard barked at her. Deviating from staring at the wall felt like a mistake. Trying her best not to move a single muscle, her eyes scanned the floor between her legs.

A menacing silhouette of a stranger shadowed the ground. Riley's heart pounded against her ribs so hard she thought they might fracture. The sound of her pulse throbbing in her ears boomed over the footsteps fading from her cell, punctuated by a high-pitched squeak and rattling slam of the cell door.

"At ease, Michaels."

Riley's arms dropped to her side, sore from holding the position. A shiver slithered down her spine as she pivoted. It felt as though all of the oxygen had left the room with the guards, and two inmates were left to battle for the next breath. Riley was met with brown eyes - the same brown eyes that dissected her every move just a few hours earlier.

A condescending smirk grew on Syke's face. Riley's remained stone cold.

"Of course, they made me bunkies with the teacher's pet," the inmate growled as she observed her new surroundings. Syke put her minimal belongings on the edge of the sink and turned the water off. She moseyed around the room with little regard for Riley's belongings. She kicked off her slippers and pointed to the cot in front of her.

"Was this one yours? I hope you don't mind. I don't sleep on top bunks."

Hours could have slipped by unnoticed. For all Riley knew, her muscles were frozen.

"I know you speak. You were talkin' up a storm in class earlier. About my dreams and whatever else." She sat up from her bunk and turned her body toward Riley.

"What? Are you scared of me?"

Fear constricted her throat, squeezing the words from her lungs, but she knew she had to say something.

"Well." Riley managed to squeak through her lips.

"Well, what?" Syke said, disoriented.

"What did you… write about?"

———

Riley wasn't sure what disappointed her more - the fact that Syke was her new "bunkie" or that none of the other inmates in the class finished their dream assignment. The moments after Syke's arrival swirled with unspoken tension. Asking about the assignment only seemed to annoy Syke even more.

After clambering to the top bunk, Riley felt a sting of isolation. Not only was her "sanctuary" invaded by the person who seemed to despise her the most, but Syke claimed the only pillow in the cell that wasn't as flat as cardboard.

Ignoring the urge to ignite a pillow fight, Riley retreated further into her shell, allowing the silence to thicken around her.

At 10:23 AM, she began to zone out as she counted each individual piece of vermiculite in the popcorn ceiling above her. 376, 377, 378…

Riley was jolted awake by the sound of a horrifying shriek.

"MICHAELS. GET DOWN FOR COUNT." A guard barked at her.

She frantically wiped a gritty film from her eyes and jumped from her top bunk. She stumbled as the clock came into focus: 12:03 PM. Three minutes past count. Shuffling out of her cell, she fell in line with the other inmates.

"I'm really sorry, sir." Riley cowardly voiced to the guard.

She scanned the faces of the inmates around her. Judging by the ferocious grimace radiating from Syke, she knew exactly what she was doing. Riley had a sour taste in her mouth from her slumber, and her stomach growled loudly. As they marched to lunch, Riley couldn't help but say something to Syke.

"Uh, hey," Riley whispered, trying to avoid being heard by the guard. "Why didn't you wake me for lunch?" Syke chuckled and groaned. She slowed her steps to inch closer toward Riley. Syke grabbed Riley's hand and squeezed twice, tensing more with each compression.

"Ah teach, I'm sorry! You looked mighty comfy up there. Didn't want to interrupt your dreaming!"

Lauren

The fluorescent light strips hummed above the inmates, radiating a sterile glow over the classroom. Two days had passed since the interrogation, though it felt like a lifetime to Riley. She channeled the negative emotions about her convoluted conversation with Detective Cho and replaced them with a familiar rhythm and routine. Teaching the G.E.D. students had become her safe haven. A room where she could detach from her fractured thoughts and help mold a second chance at a better life for the inmates.

Each woman in the program was unique. There were seven total inmates, with little to no similarity to Riley. It didn't take her long to understand each of their quirks.

Garcia was quiet and unproblematic. English was her second language, so that presented an additional challenge for Riley. Baker, Bailey, and Campbell were the rebellious bunkies who initially snubbed the program. Though their emotions had been stoic, they hadn't given any pushback since the first lesson, which they never bothered to complete. Carter had true potential. She was the only inmate who seemed to actually care about her education and was a fairly decent writer. Foster struggled with basic concepts, and though Riley continued to be patient and give extra support, the random outbursts of frustration were jarring.

Regardless of their traits, most all seemed to respond well to Riley's encouragement and teaching style.

Except for Syke.

Since their exchange about missing lunch, their cell had been an island of ice. Riley and Syke had meticulously avoided each other's gaze and any conversation at all costs. The separation felt like a bit of relief, though Riley wondered where Syke's hatred stemmed from. Her demeanor in class was somber, uninterested, and antagonizing toward the other inmates. Their interest in Riley's lessons and bettering themselves only seemed to fuel her frustration more.

Riley began reading an excerpt from the tattered textbook she found on the first day in the classroom. She hoped a debate would spark some conversation and help the inmates strengthen their deductive reasoning skills.

"Alright, everyone, today we're going to have a friendly discussion on whether you think computers should replace traditional teachers in elementary schools. Some would argue that human teachers provide a level of emotional connection that computers just don't possess. While others feel computers have so much more knowledge that it outweighs the emotional aspect. But I want to hear what your thoughts are," Riley said excitedly, closing the book and leaning back on her desk. The room stared blankly up at her until Carter spoke up.

"Computers are only useful if you know how to use them. I think they can replace some parts of schooling, but definitely not everything."

Riley's eyes twinkled with delight. "Very good point. Someone is going to have to teach you how to use the technology properly." She retorted. "Anyone else?"

Campbell immediately chimed in. "Yeah, but like, what if we combine them?"

"What the hell does that mean?" Baker said, slapping Campbell on the arm.

The guard observing the room stood up, making his presence known.

"Sorry," said Baker. "That just sounds dumb."

"Well, if you let me finish. I was gonna say that real teachers could, like, record themselves giving lessons, and the kids could play it back. That way, they never miss anything, and they don't have to take notes." Campbell rebutted, slouching back in her chair proudly.

"Oh, interesting," Riley said, intrigued by the conversation. "Not only does that provide a great resource for the kids to reference later, but you're technically not eliminating the teacher either, just introducing another format. I like it, I like it! Keep going!" She encouraged, fascinated by the varying opinions.

"Um," Garcia chimed in. "Kids...need a lot of...help? Computers cannot...answer everything?"

"She has a point. Kids are notorious for asking a hundred questions. The computer won't be able to hold their hand through it all." Riley pondered, hopefully encouraging the inmates to do the same.

"I'll tell you what!" A voice exploded from the back of the class, startling everyone. "I really wish our teacher was a damn computer right now. I'm so sick of this!" Syke yelled, smashing her hands on her desk and cracking off a piece from the edge. The guard immediately ran over to her and slammed Syke's body down before escorting her out of the classroom. The door shut, introducing fresh air into the class.

"Yoooo," Bailey teased. "Syke's definitely gettin' thrown in the SHU this time." Campbell and Baker chimed in with laughter.

"What's the SHU?" Riley asked reluctantly. The three rebels scoffed at her and continued their own banter.

44

"It stands for Special Housing Unit. Basically, solitary confinement. They make you stay in the same room for 24 straight hours, sometimes more, depending on what you did to get there. There are no windows, and the door is completely solid metal. They bring all your meals to you." Carter generously explained.

"Yeah, it does something crazy to your brain, being alone for that long," Foster chimed in. "I've only had to do it once, and I swore I would never go back."

"I dunno know what's gotten into her. She never used to be this angry," Carter said. "To be honest, she used to be really low-key."

Riley nearly choked on the lump lodged in her throat. The ringing of Syke's outburst continued to hang heavy in the air. The anticipation of blame would soon rain down upon Riley when she came face to face with Syke again. The urge to coil like a snake and disappear into the background was overwhelming.

The clock on the wall mocked her - there were still 20 minutes left of her class. Mindless chatter from the inmates morphed and swirled into haunting thoughts in Riley's head. She could feel herself start to panic. Her weak fingers managed to grab a few loose-leaf sheets, and she instructed the inmates to write down their opinions on the debate. A choir of moans filled the room, as Riley expected.

But like a dying wind, the noise soon faded into the familiar scratch of scribbling pencils. The silence didn't feel victorious, though. It felt more like a thick shroud, suffocating the already stiff atmosphere. She sat quietly in agony for what felt like hours, watching each second tick by.

"Maybe…maybe she won't blame me." Riley optimistically thought to herself, tapping her foot violently against the floor.

After some time passed, the guard who had taken Syke to solitary confinement barged back through the door, and everyone jumped. "Alright, delinquents, pencils down. Let's wrap for lunch."

———

The cell glowed with hues of yellow and orange as the sun began to set. Riley filled her afternoon with books from the library, something that reminded her of being at home. She used to speed through stories, soaking in every character, plot line, and insignificant detail. Though today, she had reread the same page six times. Her mind couldn't stop wandering away from the book. Her focus had fractured like a dropped mirror, reflecting jagged shards of Syke's scowl as she stormed out of the class earlier that day.

"I'm just going to confront her," Riley thought confidently, as the worn edges of her book danced between her fingers. She stood up from her bed to face herself in front of the foggy mirror.

"What's your problem with me?" Riley rehearsed to herself quietly. Her voice was barely a whisper at first. "Did I do

46

something to offend you? I've been nothing but invisible since we met. Is that not enough?" Riley exclaimed; her voice began to echo with each word that poured from her mouth.

"You think I like being cooped up together? I DON'T EVEN BELONG HERE!" Riley shouted as her hands pounded into the metal sink, stinging her fingers. Tears welled in her eyes.

"Ha, get a load of this." A voice called mockingly from outside of the cell. Riley's neck whipped around. "The princess finally snapped." His laughter carried down the corridor, scraping against Riley's already shredded nerves.

"Psh. Whatever," she muttered, staring into her own reflection. Outside of jail, her demeanor was always soft-spoken and the complete opposite of confrontational. She rarely ever engaged in arguments and usually had a positive spin on every situation. But today, she felt a flame ignite in her soul. She was confident and relieved that she had a plan. Her voice felt like a loaded weapon.

She knocked out a few chapters before heading to dinner. A spicy scent filled the chow hall that made Riley giddy with excitement, something that didn't happen very often anymore.

"*Oh, thank God. Something finally goes my way.*" Riley thought as she made her way to the front of the line. She was given two soft-shell tacos with something that resembled ground beef and beans. She wasn't excited about the mystery meat, though - this was the only meal that offered fresh tomato and lettuce.

Riley could write a mile-long list of things she missed from home, but one of the biggest was the vegetables from her garden. She planted everything from lettuce to carrots to watermelon. The strawberries were a hit with April, who ate them straight from the vine. Riley craved the fresh piquant taste of vegetables, and taco night was as close as she could get. She sat down at the edge of the table with her tray and fruit punch, keeping her distance from the other inmates. She immediately dove into the veggies and reminisced about the garden yield she proudly picked each year.

Dinner ended quickly. Riley was eager to return to her cell to have a quiet evening before tomorrow's unknown. One that wasn't filled with Syke's obnoxious snoring. She shuffled behind the crowd of inmates headed to her block until she reached her cell. The guard nudged her in as if she wasn't going fast enough. She stumbled over the uneven threshold.

After regaining her balance, Riley heard a chuckle that slithered through the cell. Her arms prickled with goosebumps. A shiver erupted across her skin like a thousand daddy-long legs hiding under her clothes. Slowly, her head lifted. There, in the shadowed corner, Syke loomed with her arms crossed, like she had been waiting for Riley's arrival. Though taken aback, Riley stood confidently, remembering the script she rehearsed.

"Everyone thought you went to the…" Riley paused, trying to remember what the others called it.

"You thought they'd throw me in the SHU for that? Huh. You really don't know anything about jail, do you?"

Riley was stunned. *"This wasn't part of the plan,"* she thought to herself, panicking while trying to remain strong. "What's your problem with me?" she asked firmly, her voice cracking with every other word. Syke sat motionless.

"Did she not hear me? I definitely said it loud enough, right? Should I say it again?" Riley's thoughts swirled. "I've stayed out of your way since we met. What more do you want from me?" She said, taking a few steps forward.

"What do I want from you?" Syke said, standing firmly on her feet before taking leaps toward Riley. Syke shoved Riley's shoulders into the brick wall. Arms locked, Syke brought her face as close to Riley's without their lips touching.

"I want you to come clean and tell the cops where that little girl is," she yelled. The stench of bad breath and taco meat stained the inside of Riley's nose. Syke's grip released, and she stepped back from the wall, hate fuming in her eyes.

"That's what this is about?!" Riley screamed, stepping closer to Syke, frustration fueling her newfound self-assurance. "You can't be serious. You know nothing about me or what happened. That girl was like my own daughter. I would never do anything like this." Riley stepped even closer toward her new bunkie, blind to any possible repercussions. "Keep my situation out of your mouth," she shouted, pushing Syke to the side to get up on the top bunk.

Riley tried to remain silent, but words flowed out of her mouth like a waterfall. "What the hell do you care, anyway? You definitely don't seem like the kid type. You don't seem like the anyone-but-yourself type," she said, gripping the edge of her bunk. The room reverberated with her words. Her confidence high began weaning. She fully expected to be pummeled. But to her surprise, Syke hadn't moved.

"*Maybe she's planning on how to kill me.*" Riley thought during the tense silence. "*Suffocating me in my sleep would probably be the easiest clean-up. She could make it look like a complete accident. Or maybe she'll bash my head over the sink.*"

Through all of Riley's outlandish murder scenes, Syke stood frozen, expression blank. After a few minutes, the light reflected on a single tear that fell from her cheek. Syke meandered to her bunk and curled up with her blanket like a cocoon. "*What the hell just happened?*" Riley pondered. "*That...was too easy. What did I say that made her just submit like that?*" The room remained quiet for hours.

———

The oppressive silence of the room pulsated with nervous energy. Riley counted cracks in the brick walls to pass the time, eyelids heavy from exhaustion. But adrenaline buzzed under her skin like a trapped hornet.

Syke lay unnaturally still below her. Riley could tell she was still awake because her thunderous snoring wasn't radiating through the room. Fear taunted Riley. If Syke was planning something, sleep was the perfect opportunity to strike. Just as Riley was losing the fight against exhaustion and an adrenaline crash, she was jolted by a hushed tone.

"Michaels," called Syke, cowardly. Riley paused for a few moments before responding.

"Yeah?"

"Is that girl really missing? You...you don't know where she is?" Syke asked bluntly.

"Yes," Riley said, as firm as could be while holding her breath. The room went silent again for a few minutes before Syke muttered.

"Look," Syke started, her voice shaking. "I snapped. You were an easy target, and what they've been sayin' on the news about you and the missing girl...I don't mess around when it comes to kids."

Riley was taken aback by the accusation, but she was never one to hold a grudge. Although it wasn't an apology, the sincerity in Syke's voice made it feel like one.

"I get it. I'd feel the same way. Not that I need you to believe me, but when I get out of here, I am going to do anything and everything I can to find her."

Syke shifted her weight to the opposite side, shaking the bunk.

"My little girl," Syke started, her voice oozing with pain. "She went missing almost six months ago. Disappeared from my backyard, with no clues or anything. I can't breathe without thinkin' about her. Hearing about you brought all those feelings back." Riley was stunned, unable to speak, and immediately became emotional. The animosity suddenly made sense. Riley's case was a twisted resemblance to Syke's shattered world. She thought for minutes, searching for the right thing to say.

"God. Syke, I'm so-" A familiar cadence of snoring interrupted Riley's sentiment. Holding back tears stung Riley's eyes as she gazed at a sliver of the night sky through the sad excuse for a window in their room. The silence no longer felt empty. It was filled with a common ground of sorrow and desperation for uncovering the truth of what happened to both girls.

———

Comfort was a distant memory for Riley, especially that night. Her eyes sprang open every fifteen minutes to reposition her flattened pillow or shift to the opposite side. Her dreams meshed with reality as if she were stuck in a twisted state of consciousness.

52

After battling through the night, Riley decided to start her day at 4 AM. Breakfast wasn't served until at least five, so she had time to kill. She carefully climbed down from the top bunk, hoping not to wake Syke. She peeked out the window to see dusk slowly fading into dawn. She turned on the faucet labeled "H" and prayed that it worked.

Showers had been absolutely miserable for Riley. Aside from the grime-covered floor and scentless soap bars, the water never approached lukewarm. In the two weeks she'd been at Triple C, she had only showered twice, which was out of complete necessity. She mostly gave herself sponge baths from the sink in her room. On the warmest setting, the water was always as cold as ice. Even that was more comforting than standing completely naked in a room full of strangers, gawking at her every crevice and curve.

She zoned out, staring at the running water for a few minutes before slowly making contact with her index finger. What she expected to be ice turned out to be the complete opposite.

"Ow!" Riley exclaimed, pulling her hand back quickly and checking to see if her screech woke Syke. Steam flared from the stream of water, enticing her to go back for more. The phantom of heat still stung within her finger, but she felt as if she had struck gold. Not the kind you dug for, but the kind that flowed.

"*It must be the time...*" She thought to herself. "*Everyone is still asleep, and the breakfast crew hasn't started to prep yet.*"

Relieved and excited, she cracked the cold faucet ever-so-slightly before touching the stream again. It wasn't just her hands that melted; it was her entire body. She had forgotten the relaxation warmth brought. After washing her arms and face, she realized this wouldn't last much longer.

She immediately looked to Syke, sleeping soundly, unaware of the lavishness they had access to before anyone else. Without thinking, Riley found herself walking over to her bunk. She cautiously approached closer, before lightly grazing Syke's arm. She didn't move. Riley started shaking her arm harder.

"Syke. Hey…wake up." Riley said softly. Syke started to stir before snapping awake.

"Ah! What the?" She pulled the blanket closer to her. Riley stepped back.

"Sorry to wake you, but we've got hot water." Riley stood there blankly until Syke reacted. It felt like minutes had passed, and time was running out.

"Are you…Are you messing with me?" Syke rubbed her eyes to clear her vision.

"Uh, no, look!" Riley pointed to the cloud of steam collecting in the corner of the room. Syke sprang out of bed like she had just been told she was free to go. She doused herself in the water, carelessly flinging drips around the room.

For the first time since they had met, Syke had a genuine smile on her face. Riley stood back, feeling accomplished. Syke motioned for Riley to join her. The inmates, once brutal enemies, stood side by side, embracing the rare luxury.

Just as quickly as it came, the water turned from hot to warm, from warm to cool, and then to frigid. Syke turned the water off, flailing her hands in the air to dry the excess water. "Man, Michaels…you aight." Syke said, walking past Riley and back into bed. Riley grinned, knowing this was exactly what they needed. Riley and Syke spent the hour before breakfast talking about anything and everything. Riley spoke of her writing career, her childhood growing up at the beach, and how much she missed her cat, Griddle. Syke, whose first name was Amari, spoke novels about her daughter and the life they used to have.

"I don't know if you're allowed to ask this," Riley said hesitantly, "but what are you in for? I know you said your daughter went missing, but they don't think you did it, do they?"

Amari hung her head, shaking it softly back and forth. "All of this is so fucked up. Of course, they think I did it. I was my daughter's everything. Listen, after Lauren disappeared, I became a different woman. I used to have my life straight, you know? I had a good job, friends, and a life. As soon as everything went down, I went just… crazy trying to find her." Amari started, inhaling deeply.

"Her dad and I had broken up a few months before she went missing. Our relationship turned toxic, and he threatened me with a restraining order. I had stopped taking my bipolar meds. It was just…a really hard time. When Lauren disappeared, he decided to stop cooperating with me. He didn't care nearly as much as I did. So, one night, after I had one too many trying to drown my pain, I grabbed my pistol from the safe and went to his house. My gut was tellin' me that he had something to do with all this. I broke in through a window, and I guess one of the neighbors saw and called the cops. He wasn't even home that night, but they booked me for burglary with a deadly weapon, and I've been waiting for a trial. I even tried to tell them about my girl and that I thought she might be there, but they didn't care. I was lower than dirt to them." Amari caressed her face in her hands. "It was stupid, and I regret it. But I know my girl is still out there, and just like you, I'm going to do what I gotta do to bring her home."

Amari stared into Riley's green eyes. Riley carefully placed her hand on Amari's shoulder. "Just like I'm going to find April, I'm going to find Lauren too." She immediately lunged into Riley's embrace, solidifying their connection. After wiping the tears from her eyes, Amari asked a question that Riley wasn't ready for.

"So, you've been in here for a minute now. Why has nobody bailed you out if you didn't do it? Don't you have family or friends or anyone to help you?"

Riley felt a rush of sickness churn in her stomach. The answer she wanted to scream was *no*. Her heart ached even more thinking about the family she left back home. Kendra was her only lifeline since tragedy struck a few years back, and since the incident, Riley had been completely alone.

"I...I don't have anyone on the outside anymore. April's parents were all I had. I'm still pretty new around here," Riley depressingly said.

"Yeah, but, like, you had to have family and friends from wherever you came from, right?" Amari questioned, craving the truth about Riley's past. Riley scrambled for an answer. She wasn't ready to face what truly happened.

"My family isn't around anymore." She stood up to grab a drink of water from the sink. "I'll just leave it at that," she said, cupping her hands.

"What, you kill em' or something?" Amari said, half-joking.

Riley didn't find it very amusing. "No," she said, slurping the water rather loudly to deflect the conversation.

Just then, a guard appeared in front of their cell. Riley flicked the water from her hands and turned toward the guard. "Which one of you is Riley Michaels?" The guard called into the cell. Riley took a half-step forward.

"I am?" Riley questioned, nearly wishing she wasn't.

The cell door unlocked, and the guard motioned Riley closer. "You need to come with me."

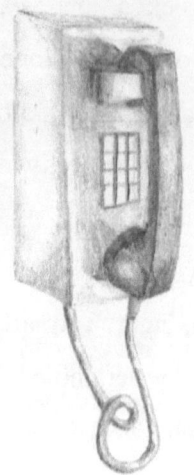

freedom from the walls

The swirl of uncertainty engulfed Riley's head. The inmates in her block taunted her as she wandered down the hall.

"*Ooooooooooh*. What did Michaels do now?" They questioned. "They probably found proof that she helped kidnap that kid!" Their voices followed Riley like a shadow, but she was fixated on where she could be headed.

When she first got to Triple C, they mentioned that she would be appointed a lawyer if she were to go to trial—maybe they were ready to meet to discuss the details of the case. It all felt so unconventional to her.

"*Why would a lawyer need to see me at nearly six in the morning?*" She thought quietly to herself.

The guard led her into an open room with seven phones attached to the wall. The cords coiled in every direction, fueling Riley's obsessive tendencies. "Number six," called the guard, sitting in the metal chair in the corner. Riley looked back toward the guard.

"Who am I supposed to be calling?" she asked.

"Here." The guard handed her a crumpled sticky note with a phone number.

"That doesn't really answer my question, but okay." Riley thought to herself as she gripped the cold payphone.

The ringing tone eerily filled the room like she was a horror movie victim. A voice abruptly answered.

"Great Escape Bail Bonds, this is Jessica. How can I help you?"

"Hello…?" She began. "This is…Riley. Riley…"

"Ah, Michaels! Yes." She exclaimed. "I've been expecting your call. Good news, Chica, you're being bailed out today."

"I'm what?" Riley was stunned, hardly able to comprehend Jessica's words.

"You know, bailed out? Like, uh, someone is paying you to leave early. You've played that one board game, right? With the "Get-Out-Of-Jail Free card? Well, it ain't free, but the card is all yours!" She said, chuckling at her silly banter.

Riley anxiously wrapped the coiled phone cord around her finger until the tip turned purple. *"Bailed out?"* She thought. Her heart fluttered with excitement, which was immediately dampened by pure confusion.

"Am I allowed to ask who did that?"

"Who did...what? Oh! Bail you out? Yeah, sorry, they want to remain anonymous. A real Jane Doe situation. They did say they would come to pick you up, though! Would be quite a shame if you had to walk home!" She laughed again. Her nonchalant attitude was starting to get under Riley's skin.

"There's nothing else for you to do other than sign the paperwork. Glad I got to deliver the good news! Have the best day!"

The phone went silent, and Riley hung it back on the hook. The guard flashed a slight side smile from the corner of his mouth.

"Alright, Riley. Hope your hand is ready. We've got a lot of paperwork to do." This was the first time a guard, or anyone in Triple C, called her by her first name.

———

It had been forty-five minutes since Riley received the strangest phone call of her life. Those minutes were completely filled with changing back into her street clothes and signing stacks of paper, allowing her to trade her cell for a promise that she would appear for her court date, which was set for May 21st.

She checked every box and signed on every dotted line as fast as she could.

Each completed sheet felt like a wall being demolished around her, leading her to the outside world. She couldn't wait to breathe fresh air, wear clothes that weren't two sizes too big, and, most importantly, do everything to find April.

Riley laid down the pen and unclenched her fist, allowing the blood to rush back to her fingertips. She slid the paper toward the guard and flashed a side smile, in hopes that was the last one.

"Alright, that's all for now. Have a seat in the waiting area."

Riley found the seat closest to the door. She held her breath, her veins pulsating in her neck, anticipating freedom being within reach. But her excitement quickly turned to nerves as familiar faces flashed in her brain.

Garcia. Baker. Campbell. Carter. Foster. Bailey. Amari.

"Would Amari know why I wasn't coming back? Would someone tell her?" Riley worried. The two of them had made such strides in such a short time.

"And what about the students? Would they still continue the program without a teacher?" These questions cascaded through her brain, revealing spots of darkness in her head.

Without thinking, she stood from her chair and walked over to the guard sitting behind the glass pane. "Excuse me?" Riley softly asked.

"Yes?" Grunted the guard.

"I still have a few books in my cell from the library. Will someone return them for me?" The guard looked dumbfounded that she even asked such a question.

"Uh, yeah. We'll take care of the books." The guard returned to her stack of paperwork. Riley thanked her and turned to walk away, but stopped to ask the question that was originally on her mind.

"Um, how do I contact someone from in here? Like, another inmate?" The guard paused what she was doing once again and looked at Riley.

"You can go online and find their SBI number. Then you can arrange a call during business hours." The guard looked at Riley as if she were saying, "Anything else?" Riley smiled and sat back down in her chair.

A few moments later, the guard answered a phone call and made direct eye contact with Riley.

"Okay, I'll let her know." The guard said, hitting the end button. Riley waited for the guard to say something, yet she went back to looking at her desk without saying a word. A sudden loud buzzing radiated through the waiting room, and a guard appeared with a manila envelope with "MICHAELS, RILEY" written in black marker. Riley's heart raced. The door in front of her chair unlocked, and the guard escorted her out. They walked quietly outside, still trapped by two barbed fences on each side.

After what felt like a marathon, they reached the final door that led to the outside of the jail. The guard handed Riley the envelope.

"This folder contains your documents and anything you had on your person before you entered the facility."

Riley took the folder, looking doe-eyed.

"I wish you the best of luck."

As quickly as the guard arrived, he disappeared back into the abyss of the jail. Riley looked at her surroundings. No walls, no barbed wire, no guards watching her every move.

Finally free, and there was no going back. She happily strutted along the paved pathway to the parking lot on the side of the building.

Nearly blinded by the bright sunlight, her skin felt like it was being hugged by the sun's rays. She closed her eyes, not out of fear, but by choice, soaking in the newfound freedom. Her brain illustrated the events she encountered over the past few weeks, flickering like she hit the rewind button. Relief tangled with unease in the pit of her stomach. Was this feeling of freedom real or just temporary? Feeling weak, her body collapsed on the curb. The uncertainty of the impending trial and April's well-being shielded her brain from her once optimistic thoughts. Her freedom felt borrowed and fragmented.

She released her grip from the folder with her name on it. She pinched the prongs and opened the flap to reveal only three items. She pulled out a tube of lip balm, something she never left the house without; her house key, which she left in the folder along with the lip balm; and stuck in the corner of the folder was a dainty silver chain, a necklace her mom had gifted to her many years ago. She wrapped the chain around her neck and gently adjusted the pendant on her chest.

Riley felt a rush of air that sent a chill down her body. She opened her eyes to reveal a big, gray tire next to her feet. Startled, she got up off the ground quickly and in front of the driver's side door stood Kendra, tears streaming down her face.

What once was a familiar face was now one of complete alarm. Riley stumbled back as the panic overtook her.

"What are you doing here?" Riley yelled, gripping her necklace for comfort.

"We can't talk here. Get in." She squeezed from her throat as her tears flowed into her mouth.

"The car? You want me to get in the car with you? Are you crazy? You're part of the reason I was here in the first place!" Riley screamed, continuing to inch away from Kendra's car.

"I'm also the reason you got out. I don't want to make a scene, especially not here. Get in the car."

Riley stopped dead in her tracks.

"Get out? Was it you? Were you the one who paid my bail?" Riley's questions flowed as if a dam had just collapsed.

"I will explain everything. Just get in the car." Kendra begged, gritting her teeth.

Riley's muscles seized as her head and heart battled. The trust Riley had for Kendra had been demolished, but if she was the person who paid her bail, she owed her at least the chance for an explanation. Knowing she needed to take this chance, she swiftly walked over to the vehicle and jumped in the passenger door. Kendra immediately locked the door and sped out of Triple C's parking lot.

Stiff as a board, it was hard to keep Riley's uneasiness contained as she sat inches away from Kendra. About five minutes away from Triple C, Kendra turned down a side road that was lined with tall, bushy trees. Kendra put the car in park but continued to look straight ahead.

"Kendra, I really need you to…"

"I heard everything." Kendra interrupted.

"You…you heard…what?"

"You had your interrogation a few days ago. I was there."

Riley's memories flooded with images of the interrogation room, and a spotlight shined on the fuzzy paned glass and the three silhouettes. She audibly gasped, knowing how torturous listening to the events of that night must have been for Kendra.

"That night, I couldn't sleep after listening to what really happened, so I went to your house. I sat in my car staring at your front yard for two hours. I don't know what possessed me to do it, but I got out. I remember you telling me that you kept a spare key in the turtle planter next to your door. So, I grabbed it and went inside."

"Why?" The only word Riley managed to eke out.

"I needed to know you were telling the truth. As soon as I opened the door, I looked for my pair of shoes - the ones you were wearing that night when the car ran over your foot."

"Oh God, not this again," Riley thought to herself.

"When I held up the shoe to the light, I saw the muddy tire marks across the top, clear as day. And I broke down crying."

At this point, Riley didn't have any words left. She watched Kendra become overwhelmed by emotion and decided to let her have her moment.

"Riley, you're the only one who knows her as well as I do. I know that she's out there. We just have to find her."

"I'm so sorry," Riley professed, pulling her head into Kendra's shoulder. Kendra squeezed her reassuringly. She pulled back to look into Kendra's brown eyes. "Now, let's go find April."

On the ride, Riley insisted on formulating a plan to find April, but Kendra knew Riley needed to decompress to have a level head. With some resistance, Riley agreed and turned the conversation elsewhere. She told Kendra stories of the food she ate, the books she read, and the people she met. She told her all about the fragmented relationship with Syke, the G.E.D. students, and the refreshing feeling of having hot water for the first time in over two weeks. Though still guarded, Kendra was empathetic to what Riley had been through.

After hearing about the awful meals, Kendra stopped at their favorite fast food joint, the one they frequented every Sunday as a start-of-the-week pick-me-up.

Riley was overwhelmed by the smell of fresh, oily French fries and griddled onions on her burger. She took a bite, and her taste buds exploded. Flavor, once a forgotten memory, was now overwhelming and plentiful. Riley managed to squeeze a quick "thank you" between each bite, hoping that Kendra fully understood what this meant to her. It wasn't long before Riley's stomach started to ache. After not eating a proper meal for weeks, just a few bites were enough to make her stomach protrude.

She wrapped up the remains of her burger and fries and slid them back into the brown paper bag. Riley stared at Kendra, who was focused on merging onto the highway. She turned to look out the window and was mesmerized by the cloud formations and the vibrant color of the trees. Her head slowly met the glass, and with each bump and vibration of her seat, she felt herself drifting to sleep.

———

Riley was jolted awake by Kendra shifting the car into park. She sat up quickly, forgetting where she was for a moment, before recognizing a familiar stoop.

"Welcome home," Kendra said, unbuckling. Though normally groggy after a nap, Riley surged as if she'd just had two espresso shots. She unbuckled and jumped out of the car with her envelope.

The women stood side by side for a moment before heading up the steps. Riley pulled out her house key from the folder and slowly opened the lock. The door busted open, and there, sitting in the middle of the floor, was Griddle. She barely made it through the doorway before collapsing into tears. Griddle trotted over and nuzzled between Riley's knees. His fur was just as soft as she remembered, but was now riddled with small mats toward his tail.

"He was almost out of food and water when I came a few days ago. I refilled everything, even the litter that was overflowing. I'm sorry I didn't check on him sooner," Kendra said, dejected.

"I guess that's what self-feeders are for, huh? They really come in handy when you disappear," Riley said with a coy attitude, fighting back tears. "Thank you for doing that. I'm just glad he's okay."

Griddle was super-glued to Riley as she made her way through the living room. Everything was exactly as she'd left it, down to the handful of popcorn that spilled on the floor as Kendra knocked on the door that night. Even with her body tensing, Riley attempted to remain calm while in Kendra's presence.

"I'd like to get changed," Riley said, almost asking Kendra's permission. She motioned Riley to the bedroom and was quickly followed by Griddle, who snuck through the door frame.

"I'll just be a moment," she called to Kendra. She was sitting on the couch in the living room.

She stood motionless in her room. Her sheet lay scattered across her bed, reminiscent of the last sleep she took. A noticeable Griddle-sized divot was in the center of her pillow. She gave her furry friend a pet on the head and quickly rummaged through her closet for her favorite sunshine yellow sweatshirt and a pair of jeans. Normally, she would opt for sweats, but something about starchy jeans made her feel human again.

Being between the four walls of her bedroom felt like she was in a dream sequence. There were no guards barking orders, no inmates taunting her, just the calming silence of her olive-green room adorned with abstract paintings.

Riley joined Kendra in the living room and sat in her favorite spot on the couch. Kendra spent the next hour filling her in on everything that had happened since April's disappearance. Small search committees were formed, scouring the city for any traces of April they could find. Kendra went days without sleeping, knowing there had to be some small, insignificant detail that she missed. Even with everything Kendra had told her, Riley couldn't shake a question that kept replaying in her mind.

"Kendra, where has Quincy been during all of this?" Riley asked reluctantly. Kendra shifted her body on the couch nervously.

"He...doesn't do well with uncomfortable situations," Kendra said, hiding her gaze. "He'll do anything he can to distract himself. He went back to work shortly after she disappeared. Everyone processes differently, I guess." She hung her head lower until her knees covered her face. "He doesn't know that I did this." She fiddled with her wrists.

"Did what?" Asked Riley.

"Bailed you out."

Riley sank into the back of the couch, eyes wide with fear. "You didn't tell him?!" She hoped this was a cruel joke.

"He's been so unreasonable. He's insistent that you're connected to this somehow, and I don't blame him, I guess. I was convinced you were, too. But I came to my senses after everything I heard. He still wouldn't listen when I told him it couldn't have been you." Kendra confessed tearfully.

"So...when is he coming home?" Riley asked.

"Uh," Kendra paused, nervously looking around the room. "Tonight."

"Tonight?" Riley questioned. "What's your plan? I can't just hide here to avoid being seen by him. We need to be out there looking for April!" Riley said aggressively, sending Kendra into a panic.

"I DON'T KNOW!" Kendra shouted, making the hair on Griddle's back stand straight up. She stood up from the couch and paced around the living room, her hands covering her face. "I don't know anything anymore. I knew you had nothing to do with what happened, and you would be the *only* person dedicated enough to helping me find her. So, I did what I had to do." Kendra stopped pacing, turned to Riley, and placed her hands on the back of the couch. "Well, you're up," she faltered. "I'm at a loss. Please say something, anything."

Riley paused for a moment, terrified to say the wrong thing. Her mind swirled like a racehorse circling the track. She knew this rescue mission lay completely on her shoulders.

"I...I just want to find my little girl. I just need to know that she's safe," Kendra pleaded.

"Hm, where's my phone?" Riley intensely scanned the room.

"Wh...What?" Kendra's voice shuddered with confusion.

"My phone," Riley said, jumping up from the couch. "I need to make a call." She rushed to the bedroom to find her phone still plugged in on her bedside table. Kendra slowly walked down the hallway and rested against the doorframe.

"So, who are you planning to call?" Kendra asked as curiosity lifted her tone.

"The inmate I was telling you about, Amari, her daughter, went missing six months ago. She just vanished from her backyard.

I want to know every detail from that day and see if anything can connect these stories together." Kendra wiped her tears as her body recoiled at the idea of another missing girl.

They quickly walked back into the living room as Riley turned her phone back on. As the phone came back to life, an adorable photo of Griddle flashed on the lock screen. Notifications and messages began to pour in—a flood of disparaging news articles mentioning her by name and derogatory texts from concerned childhood friends and neighbors filled her screen. The thought of speaking to anyone but Amari was overwhelming.

She dismissed them all and searched online for how to contact an inmate at Triple C. Before she left, she remembered the guard saying that she needed some sort of identification number to talk to them.

She scoured the internet, fending off alerts like mosquitoes on a summer day. Finally, she found an inmate database where she could enter the inmate's full name, which would give them details about their history, including the SBI number. She grabbed a pen from her bedside table and wrote the number in the palm of her hand. 875222. She searched for the jail's number and dialed it as quickly as she could. The line rang three times before someone finally answered.

"Clarendon Correctional Center, how can I direct your call?"

"Hi, my name is Riley Michaels, and I need to speak with an inmate immediately."

the storm

The operator firmly explained to Riley that she needed to be placed on an approved call list. Then, she would have to add funds to her account, and if the inmate was receptive to the call, she would receive a call from them. As soon as the line went dead, Riley added money to her account, and the waiting began.

Two hours went by. Still no calls.

Kendra sat uncomfortably on the floor, hugging one of Riley's couch pillows. Riley had been pacing the floor, staring at her blank phone screen.

"What do you think calling this, Syke girl, is going to help anyway?" Kendra condescendingly asked. Riley slowly turned to look at her.

"She's been through this situation before. I just thought-"

Riley's phone suddenly exploded with vibrations that shook the table, and her ringtone blared through the room. She lunged toward the table to answer it.

"He...Hello?" Her voice cracked with nervous energy.

"YOU ARE RECEIVING A CALL FROM AN INMATE WITHIN CLARENDON CORRECTIONAL CENTER. TO ACCEPT THIS CALL, PLEASE PRESS ONE NOW. TO DECLINE THIS CALL, PLEASE HANG UP."

Riley carefully pressed one, petrified she was going to end the call by accident. Music played as she waited to hear Amari's voice. The phone was glued to the side of her head. If she heard the hold music loop one more time, she was going to have an aneurysm.

"What's taking so long!" Riley shouted into the abyss of smooth jazz as she paced up and down the hallway.

Riley pressed her back up against the wall and slid down until she was sitting. She unstuck the phone from her ear, clicked the speakerphone button, and put it on the floor.

The room was filled with the same repetitive saxophone. Griddle seemed to be the only one who enjoyed the tunes. He nuzzled the phone so aggressively that it nearly flipped over. Suddenly, the music stopped, and Riley was terrified his overzealous nudge ended the call. She frantically picked the phone up before hearing a strong "Hello?"

Riley took a deep breath. "Amari?"

"Michaels? Oh wow. They actually let you out! They didn't tell me anything!"

"Kendra…paid my bail," Riley said, still stunned.

"Like, April's mom, Kendra? She's the person who called for you? What'd she do that for? That doesn't make any sense," Amari questioned.

"I can explain later. Listen, I don't have a lot of time. I need to know more about the day Lauren disappeared."

Amari paused. "My Lauren? Why? I already told you everything I know."

"Look, it can't just be some coincidence that both of our girls go missing within a year. I'm looking for clues…absolutely anything that can help us solve this mess. Maybe they're connected, maybe not, but I need somewhere to start."

Though reluctant, she depicted everything from the day Lauren vanished with excruciating detail. Riley scrambled to find paper and a working pen to take notes.

Amari was washing dishes at the sink in her kitchen. She watched out the window at Lauren, who was nearly two at the time, playing outside in her fenced-in backyard. She bounced back and forth, from picking flowers and weeds to rolling a ball up and down the yard. Amari remembered being startled by her dogs aggressively barking out the front window.

She turned around for only a few moments to calm them down. When she came back, she returned to her dishes. Only this time, Lauren couldn't be seen from the window. Amari opened the back door and called for her, but was met with only leaves rustling in the wind. Gentle calls of Marco Polo turned to absolute panic and sheer terror when Lauren didn't answer back. Amari sprinted back into the house to call the police when-

"YOU HAVE 15 SECONDS REMAINING ON THIS CALL." An automated voice interrupted.

"No, no, no, no! I need more time!" Riley screamed.

"I'll call you again tomorrow, and I can finish up the story. It's not like I'm going anywhere!"

"Okay…Okay please do. First thing." Riley said, calming herself down. "WAIT. I need your address! Quick!"

"370 Spruc…"

The line went dead.

Riley lowered the phone from her ear and chucked it across the room, landing on the carpet just before the kitchen. Kendra, who was pacing, looked stunned.

"What happened?" She said, picking the phone up from the floor.

"The line went dead. She said she would call me back tomorrow." Riley said dejectedly, falling to the ground.

"I still don't know if the cases are connected, and that was my only." Streams of tears fell from her eyes. "But that's not going to stop me."

Riley stood up and walked over to the front door to slip on her shoes. "I'm going to be outside for a bit. You staying in here?" Riley asked as she opened the door. Kendra slowly nodded, confused at Riley's sudden burst of energy.

The porch creaked with each step she took as she made her way outside. Looking out at her yard, she analyzed the same spot where the Buick drove up - the same divots in the soil that collected puddles of water that night. "I bet the cops didn't even take pictures of these." She scoffed. There had to be something, anything she could do. She closed her eyes, breathed in the warm spring air, and replayed the events from that night, going through each motion.

Riley stayed outside for nearly two hours, going back and forth from her porch to her driveway. Kendra stood watch from the living room window. Her eyes bounced as if she were watching a tennis match. Riley lay down in the middle of her lawn, eyes locked on the clouds rushing through the air. She saw shapes that resembled a fire-breathing dragon lying on its belly, a little boy playing the trumpet, and a tall drink with a paper umbrella. Her mouth salivated at the thought of a strawberry smoothie. Growing up by the ocean, the thought of anything tropical put her mind at ease. Her fantasy was interrupted by a familiar noise, her phone ringing.

"Riley!" Kendra called from the porch. "You need to answer this!" Riley jumped up and sprinted to the steps. Before reading the caller ID, she answered.

"Hello? This is Riley."

"This is an automated message for MICHAELS, RILEY, from the court office of Clarendon Hills. Your court date has been changed from MAY 21st to MAY 28th, promptly at 11 AM in courtroom 15 before Judge Charleen Grier. It is of utmost importance that you arrive to court on time. Failure to do so will result in a warrant being issued for your arrest."

Riley held her chest tightly.

"To hear this message again, please press one now."

Riley ended the call.

"Well, who was that?" Kendra said, stepping closer to Riley. She slid her phone into her pocket and sat on the steps of her porch.

"They reset the court date. We have twenty-one days. That's it." Riley buried her face in her hands. Kendra sat next to her and rubbed her back.

"And now I have to get a lawyer!"

"Listen," Kendra started. "We can figure this out tomorrow. Quincy will be home soon and will be wondering where I am. I think you'll have a better chance of finding her with a clear head. Go inside, make some tea, and read a few books. Tomorrow is a new day."

Riley knew how much courage it took Kendra to say that, so she didn't dare contest it.

"You're right. It's been a long day. I think I might turn in early to get a head start tomorrow."

"Good plan. I'll be in touch. Unless it's an emergency, I wouldn't call or text me…just in case he's around." Riley stood up and grabbed Kendra's hand to pull her up. They embraced, and Kendra walked back to her car. Riley went inside and tried to work through her anxiety of only having three weeks to find April.

———

For the next several hours, Riley did everything to think about anything other than April. She reread her favorite novel, binged her favorite rom-coms, and made her comfort meal, pasta carbonara. But her soul was still desperate for answers. Just as the sun fully set, she walked into her bedroom and stood before her desk, staring at her charging laptop.

"I'll just…do a little light research," she thought to herself, slowly sitting down in her chair. *"Then I'll head to bed."* Griddle promptly jumped onto her lap and refused to move. She zoned out to the blinking line in the search bar, anxiously deciphering what to type first.

She finally searched "Lauren Syke Clarendon Hills IL," and immediately, her results were flooded with missing person reports, public forum search committees, articles regarding the disappearance, Syke's mugshot, and pictures of Lauren when she was an infant.

"What a beautiful girl." Looking at a picture of Lauren, it was easy to admire how her unusually natural blonde hair contrasted against her darker complexion.

Page after page confirmed the same story that Amari told her earlier that day, and nothing more. There were no additional leads or clues as to where Lauren may be or how this could connect to April's case. The attention seemed to fade just mere weeks after her disappearance, making Riley sick to her stomach.

"How could they just give up?" Riley thought, simmering with anger. The room grew darker as she continued to scroll, the computer screen becoming the only source of light in the room. Riley was so intensely focused that she didn't blink for minutes at a time. Her eyes stung from her seemingly useless research.

She rested her head on her hand and slowly noticed it slip from exhaustion, and a jolt ran through her body. Before long, Riley lay her head down on her keyboard.

"Just for a minute," she thought before drifting unconscious.

———

Riley awoke to a sun glaring through her bedroom window. Blinking profusely to adjust to the brightness, she slowly sat up and wrapped herself in a fluffy blue and white floral robe before walking down the hall to the kitchen. Overwhelmed by the smell of bacon, she perked up, knowing breakfast was right around the corner.

"Since when have you had the urge to cook me breakfast on a Saturday?" Riley called into the kitchen.

"And who says I'm making this for you?" Riley's mother, Lauri, quickly retorted with a goofy grin. Riley rolled her eyes as she peeked over her mom's shoulder to get a closer look at the bubbling bacon.

"There's no way I'm letting you eat all of that! You'll be sick!" Riley joked, walking toward the window. Her expectations of a bright blue sky and white fluffy clouds were dashed by the sight of dark, heavy swirls in the distance.

"Was it supposed to storm today?" Riley peeked through the dust-covered blinds.

"Hmm, not that I know of," Lauri said as she flipped the crispy bacon onto a paper towel to drain. Riley sneakily snagged a piece just before getting smacked on the hand. She stuck her tongue out at her mom and headed into the living room.

She flopped on the couch and turned on the TV. The weather channel filled the room with a breaking story.

"According to local meteorologists, this could be one of the worst storms Bowers Beach has ever seen!"

"Bad weather? Here?" Riley thought to herself. They haven't seen a drop of rain this entire season, let alone a category-four hurricane.

"Ma, you hearing this?" Riley called back toward the kitchen.

"We suggest that for the next 48 hours, you stay away from all doors and windows. Though evacuation is not mandated yet, we will keep you updated when more information becomes available."

"Oh, I'll believe it when I see it," Lauri said sarcastically. "You know, they make these stories up so people go buy more groceries. The station probably needed some extra ratings this week." Lauri rolled her eyes while she munched on a piece of bacon. "It's probably nothing."

"I don't know, Mom. This looks pretty serious. Maybe we should head into the city for the weekend," Riley said, popping up from the couch. "I'm gonna get a better look outside." Riley's mom shrugged her shoulders and continued making breakfast.

Riley slipped on a pair of pale blue gardening boots and walked out the front door. The sky, once bright blue, was mixed with a muted gray. The clouds were heavy with moisture as they rolled in closer toward her home. Just then, lightning began to flash in every direction, and the wind toppled her over on the sidewalk. Her knee scraped against the pavement and began to bleed.

"*Where did this come from?*" Riley thought, trying to cement her shoes to the ground. The trees were nearly horizontal, being pushed by the heavy winds. Rain and hail poured from the sky, but miraculously, she stayed completely dry as if she were holding an umbrella.

Without time to question it, the sky turned pitch black, and another gust of wind came. Riley heard a loud crash that ruptured her eardrums. Holding her ears in agony, she turned around, terrified, to find her childhood home collapsed into a pile of rubble.

"MOM!" She screamed, trying to run toward the house. But with every step she took, the house began moving farther away until it was just a blip in the distance.

Riley was surrounded by darkness. The trees, the sky, the clouds - all vanished. She began to weep, mourning her mother, who surely perished in her home. Just then, she heard a familiar noise. She looked around, wondering where it came from. She wiped the tears from her eyes and the snot from her nose.

In the distance, a light began to shine over a building. She tried getting closer, but her body kept her from advancing forward. This was a building she had seen before. A big red logo was plastered on the front entrance. Even when squinting, she couldn't make out the name.

But the noise, that familiar noise, was coming from this building. Riley started to panic as she realized the sounds vibrating in her ears were April giggling like she was being tickled. Riley started running toward the building as fast as her legs could go.

"APRIL!" She screamed, hoping someone, anyone, would hear her. She ran for what felt like hours, but the building kept getting smaller and smaller and smaller until...

"*Meow,*" Griddle said, nudging Riley's head. She lay still. "*MEOW,*" he said again, nibbling her arm.

"APRIL!" Riley screamed, springing up from her computer into a pitch-black room. Tears streamed down her cheeks and puddled on her keyboard. She wiped them with her sleeve before realizing small crumbs from her keyboard were stuck to her face.

She checked her watch. 2:47 AM. After reassuring Griddle that everything was fine, she slinked into her bed, hoping the evening of terror was over. This recurring nightmare of her mother's death haunted her.

Though the dream seemed outlandish, some of the events were, unfortunately, true. There really was a storm set to hit Bowers Beach, and they were anticipating an evacuation. Riley begged her mother to go, but she wouldn't listen. She was stubborn, after all.

Having gone through many false alarms in the past, this one didn't seem to faze her. But reluctantly, Riley left without her for the weekend and returned to her home in shambles with Lauri still trapped inside.

Although this dream would rear its ugly head from time to time, it was nearly always the same. But the dream she had awoken from tonight was different. Riley grabbed her journal from her bedside table to describe the details, especially of the building. What was so significant about that place, and what was April doing there?

swing set

The sound of purring rang in Riley's ear. Griddle's tail swished on Riley's nose as he sat nearly on top of her head. "Alright! Enough already!" She snapped. Lying still for a moment, she forgot that she was home in her own bed, and not in the jail cell that had consumed her life for the past two weeks.

Her back cracked as she rose from her sheets. Trying her best not to disturb the sleeping prince, she crawled out of bed. The clock read 10:04 AM. Shocked that she slept in that long, she grabbed her phone from the desk. Multiple missed texts and calls from Kendra illuminated her screen. Riley put the phone down and decided to freshen up before calling her back.

She shuffled over to the bathroom to find her makeup and hair care products collecting dust. Her eyes locked on her appearance in the mirror.

Dark bags cascaded under her eyes. Her hair was greasy and misplaced. Oil spots covered her face near her nose and chin. Riley looked like a shell of herself.

Her palms rubbed her eyes aggressively, hoping the gray circles would magically disappear. She ran her fingers through her hair, getting caught in knots as she combed through each strand.

Riley walked over to the shower and turned the water on as hot as it could go. Steam began to billow in the bathroom as she disrobed and entered the shower.

———

After quickly showering and running a straightener through her hair, Riley felt like a person again. Her wet towels hung on the rack to air dry, and the once-lonely haircare products breathed new life into her locks. She slinked back into her bedroom and grabbed her phone to read the texts from Kendra.

> *"Hey! What's your plan for today?"* 8:23 AM
> *"Just checking in...are you up yet?"* 9:07 AM
> *"...Hello? Are you ok?"* 9:34 AM

Riley typed as fast as her fingers could go.

"Good morning. Sorry – I had a horrible night of sleep. Just woke up. Trying to get my game plan together. I'll keep you posted." 10:46 AM

Riley thought for a moment before dialing the number for Triple C to see how early inmates were allowed to make calls. The busy signal sounded in her ear.

"Hmm, that's odd," Riley thought to herself, ending the call. She redialed the number and received the same tone. "Ummm. Okay…now what?"

She walked into the living room and saw the pad of notes from her call with Amari on the table.

- Kitchen Window
- Dogs Barking in Front
- Lauren Missing
- Called Police
- 370 Spru...

"I'm tired of waiting for everyone to help me. I can do this myself!" Riley stared down at the incomplete address in frustration. "Spruce? Sprut? Sprull?" She whipped out her phone and clicked the last search saved on her account.

The same articles and news reports filled her screen, just as they had the previous night. Only this time, she wasn't looking for information about the disappearance; she was looking for an address, a town...anything.

She clicked on an article that looked like it had been written by a local news station. Riley copied the name and searched for it.

"Ah, it's a Naperville news station. That's not far from here!" Riley felt a rush of hope as she typed in 370 "Spru", Naperville. Sure enough, a Zillow listing popped up for 370 Sprulette Road in Naperville, Illinois. She feverishly typed the address into Google Maps.

"Ah-ha!" She screamed, startling Griddle, who was strutting into the room. "This is it! There's the bay window off the back of the house, and the swing set in the backyard! This is it!" Riley said, jumping up from her seat and twirling.

Her excitement quickly faded. Even though she found the house, that didn't mean anything, but it was all that she had.

Riley quickly got dressed and skipped into the kitchen, feeling the most energy she had in weeks. She looked in her pantry for something quick to eat. Her face turned sour as she picked up a container of extremely moldy croissants. *"Ooookay..."* Riley thought, tossing them in the trash. She ultimately landed on a chocolate chip granola bar. She slipped on her shoes, grabbed her car keys, and headed out the door.

Though the air was slightly chilled, the rays of the sun illuminated her skin, reminiscent of the feeling of summer. She took a deep breath before jumping off the porch, skipping all three stairs. She opened her car door and flopped into the driver's seat. As the seatbelt clicked, she queued up her GPS. It would take her approximately 26 minutes to reach Amari's home.

For the entire ride, Riley sat in silence. Since arriving home, she realized how underappreciated the sound of nothingness actually was to her.

"Your destination is on the right," called Riley's GPS. A small, one-story home grew closer. It was cased in graham cracker colored siding and a dark black roof. The door was a bright red shade, reminiscent of lipstick. Small bunches of flowers haphazardly lined the entryway, leading up to overgrown rose bushes by the front door. Tangled vines of ivy crawled up the side of the house.

From what Amari told her back in Triple C, her mother was taking care of the home. The driveway was empty, which made Riley a bit nervous that she wasn't home. But even with a few reservations, she marched up the concrete steps with confidence, which quickly faded into fear and uncertainty. Noticing the doorbell was covered in blue painter's tape, she was forced to knock on the wooden door.

She fidgeted with the end of her shirt and analyzed the cracks in the concrete to distract herself. Feeling unprepared, Riley rehearsed what she wanted to say in her head, but her words continued to melt away like wet cotton candy. Before she could fully compose her first thought, the door swung open, and a woman in her mid-sixties peeked out.

"I'm not interested," Amari's mother said angrily, almost slamming the door.

"Oh, I-I'm-" Riley stuttered.

"Spit it out, girl!" She said, just stopping short of closing the door.

Riley stood confidently. "I'm Riley Michaels. I'm a friend of Amari's."

"So what? Amari got herself a prison girlfriend, I see?"

Riley stared back at her, confused. "Prison girlfriend? No, no, you don't understand."

"Then get to the point, copperhead. I don't have all day!" Amari's mother said bluntly.

"Look, lady, you need my help. I'm trying to find Lauren!" Riley twitched her fingers, containing her anger.

The woman's eyes bulged. The cigarette fell from her mouth. She grabbed the edge of the door for balance. Her stance buckled.

"You know about...Lauren?" She asked concernedly. Lauren's name lingered heavily in the air for a few moments.

"Yes, and my little girl was taken too."

The rest of her sentence died in her throat. The blood drained from the woman's face, leaving a mask of worry and confusion. Without saying a word, she opened the door and invited Riley in. She stepped in cautiously.

The walls were lined with baby pictures of Lauren. She stopped to look at a picture of her and Amari on the beach. Lauren couldn't have been more than 6 months old.

Her golden skin shimmered from the sun's rays, and her blonde curls had just begun sprouting. Her chunky legs and chubby cheeks reminded her of April.

Riley maneuvered through the hallway, the aging hardwood floor creaking with each step she took. The house was exactly as Amari described it, and as soon as the kitchen came into view, Riley was immediately drawn to the bay window overlooking the backyard.

"I'm Rita, by the way. I moved in after...everything happened. Amari couldn't handle being alone; honestly, neither could I. Then she lost her mind, and" she paused. "Can you blame her?" She said, stumbling into the kitchen with tears in her eyes.

She was stopped only by the kitchen sink. She gripped the edges of the countertop and gazed out the back window. "None of this makes any sense," Rita said. "I have racked my brain for the past six months trying to track her down. Lauren is just...gone."

Riley's heart pulsed to a frantic rhythm. The worst scenarios flickered behind her closed eyelids. Across the kitchen, Rita collapsed into a chair next to the island.

"I don't know what good it's gonna do by having you look around. But by all means, go for it." Rita said, defeated.

"I don't...really know why I'm here either, truthfully." Riley approached Rita and sat beside her on the floor.

"I'm sure you've seen the news. April Emery Fellowes is..."

"I KNEW YOU LOOKED FAMILIAR!" Rita shouted, jumping up from her chair. "You. You..." Rita backed away from Riley.

"I didn't do it!" Riley immediately chimed in. "The news made it look like what happened was intentional, and that couldn't be farther from the truth," she pleaded. "If I did it, they wouldn't have let me out. I wouldn't be here right now!"

Rita began to relax her tense posture. "Yeah, okay. I'm sorry. They've been blasting your name on every channel. Makes it easy to assume." Riley caught sight of the backyard again and noticed the swings swishing back and forth in the breeze.

"Have you heard from Amari today? I don't think the phones were working this morning." Riley asked, eyes locked on the curly slide and monkey bars.

94

"No. We got into an argument a few weeks ago, and I haven't heard from her since. She started spiraling again. It happens every few weeks." Rita said while rubbing her temples.

"Spiraling?" Riley questioned.

"She's convinced her baby daddy has something to do with this. She just won't let it go." Rita said in a frustrated tone.

"Yeah, she told me a bit about that."

"Well, I'm sick of hearing it! He's a bit of a ditz, but he's not a bad guy, and definitely not capable of anything like this. He had a nice upbringing, you know? He just fell in with the wrong crowd as he got a little older. Drugs and whatnot. But he's been clean ever since the baby was born, or so he told me. Maybe I'm just gullible, but I told Amari she needs to let it go and that this wasn't his fault. Guess that set her off even more, cause it's been weeks since she's called."

Riley laid her hand on Rita's shoulder. "I'm really sorry this is happening to you," Riley said genuinely, watching the pain vibrate in Rita's eyes. Rita flashed a small smile before focusing her attention on the floor.

Riley pondered for a moment before standing up and walking toward the back door. "May I?" Riley asked before gripping the door handle. Rita shooed Riley, and she immediately stepped outside. The warm breeze gently lifted the hair from her shoulders.

As she examined her surroundings, she noticed a chaotic mess of stray bottles and windblown trash lining the perimeter. The yard itself was decently maintained. Newly planted trees boasted vibrant green leaves and white buds on the verge of blooming. Unable to resist her need for tidiness, Riley began picking up the garbage.

She walked over to the swing set and ran her fingers across the nylon ropes holding the baby swing. She imagined Lauren happily trying her best to pump her little legs, hoping her feet would touch the stars.

A smile consumed her expression as Amari gave her an extra boost.

But the fantasy dissipated just as quickly as it started, and Riley was left with two empty swings. She continued picking up trash around the playset when a small slip of paper caught her eye, barely poking out of the sandbox.

"I wonder if someone's trash can blew over. How much more can there be?" Riley questioned. She reached for the paper, gently shaking the sand from the inside of the folds. It was riddled with wrinkles and slightly damp. She unveiled the paper to find a receipt from September of last year. Riley lost herself in the insignificant details of the print.

She lowered the receipt, almost putting it back in her pocket, but a small electric shock raced through her nerves. She slowly lifted the paper and locked eyes on the store logo at the top. "Healix..." Riley managed to squeeze out, the words whisked away quickly in the wind. Her fingertips felt like ice as she struggled to grasp the receipt.

It was the logo on the building she saw in her dream from the night before. She knew she had seen it before. It was the pharmacy just a few blocks from her house. She had never been in but had passed by a few times. Why was this suddenly showing up in her dream? And what are the odds that this receipt from months ago ended up here? She pulled out her phone and quickly searched for the closest Healix to Amari's house.

"*Hmm...it's the one near my house.*" Riley thought. She pondered for a moment after realizing she had cleaned the entire yard. She slowly walked back up to Amari's home, shoving the receipt in her pocket. Rita was waiting at the back door.

"Thank you for letting me look around. I'm going to be heading back home now," Riley said with a smile, trying not to confuse her.

"Did you find...anything?" Rita asked, unsure of what the possible answer could be. Riley thought for a moment. The dream receipt seemed majorly insignificant, so she chose to keep it to herself.

"No, I didn't. But that doesn't mean I'm going to stop looking."

Rita shockingly lunged toward Riley and squeezed her. "Thank you," Rita whispered into Riley's ear, maintaining her grip. Riley thanked her for letting her look and walked back to her car.

"If you hear from Amari, can you please tell her to call me?" Rita shouted from her porch. Riley gave her a thumbs up as she opened her car door. As soon as she sat down, she texted Kendra:

"Hey – I need you to come over as soon as you can. I'll explain when you get there." 12:15 PM

———

The ride home was uneventful and felt like an eternity. The songs on the radio were muffled by the thoughts exploding in Riley's head.

She pulled into her driveway to see Kendra sitting on her front porch waiting for her. She quickly hopped out of the car, and Kendra stood up.

"Hey, I got your text. Where did you go? Did you find anything? Who were you with?" Kendra eagerly called from across the yard. Riley stayed silent until she got closer. Riley fumbled with her keys before unlocking the door.

"Hello? Did you hear me?" Kendra questioned. Riley grew frustrated, not with Kendra, but with herself. She couldn't stop thinking about the receipt. It was just a dream, about a building in her hometown - how could this fit into April's story? Riley opened the door and kicked off her shoes. Kendra trailed behind her.

"Riley, you've gotta tell me what's going on..." Kendra said, following Riley like a puppy.

After making up her mind, Riley quickly turned around, holding the receipt in her hand.

"Uh, you went shopping?" Kendra asked nervously, examining the paper. "You went shopping last September?" Kendra said, confused.

"I had a dream last night," Riley said, grabbing the paper back and shaking it in front of Kendra.

"About...this receipt?"

"It was the recurring dream about my mom dying, the one I told you about. But this dream was different. It didn't end like it normally did. It ended with April laughing and giggling, walking into a building." Riley said, eyes bulging.

"Okay...? I have dreams about April every night. What does that have to do with this weird receipt? Where did you even get this anyway?" Kendra questioned. Her reaction made Riley recoil like a threatened snake.

"I feel a bit silly now, even asking you to come over to talk this through with me. But I've never had a dream about April before. Her laugh was so strong, like she was in the same room as me." Riley continued. "This receipt was nestled in Lauren's sandbox, Amari's daughter, the one that went missing last year, a- and I saw this logo in my dream! There-there was trash all over the yard, so it could have been a coincidence?" Riley said, beginning to second-guess herself.

"Hang on," Kendra said, stepping back frustratedly. "You went where?" Her voice rose, snatching the receipt back from Riley's hand.

"I went to Amari's house. Don't ask me why because I don't have an answer. I kept thinking about Lauren disappearing, too, and…" Kendra put her hand up to stop her while examining the receipt.

"Riley, I know you and this girl bonded or whatever, and you always want to help everyone. But April needs to be your focus."

Riley was a bit taken aback. Couldn't Kendra see how much energy she was putting into finding her, especially when she had nothing to go on? Nevertheless, Riley shook it off and focused again on the receipt. Kendra snatched the receipt from her hands.

"This is from the drug store down the street, not even close to Amari's house. This is the same building April went into in my dream. Isn't that just a little bit…weird?"

100

Kendra stared blankly, avoiding eye contact with Riley.

"Yeah..." Riley started, flopping down on the couch. "I knew it was a lost cause. I'm sorry I asked you to come over." Riley buried her head in her pillow. After a few moments of awkward silence, Riley looked up to see Kendra frozen, except for her hands, which were trembling slightly.

"You okay?" Riley asked, confused. Kendra looked up and locked eyes with Riley.

"Uh, yeah," Kendra said awkwardly. "It's just, this is...from Quincy's pharmacy."

a spiders silk

Riley lay perfectly still on the couch and watched the ceiling fan cord swish. The gentle winds from the blades made it sway with each rotation, like a palm tree in the breeze. The receipt that was once glued to Riley's hand was now crumpled on the table. What felt like a glimmer of a lead turned into a shadow of confusion and doubt.

"*It was just a dream. It means nothing. Let it go.*" Riley replayed in her head. Kendra sat quietly on the floor in the corner - April's toy corner. She clung to April's favorite stuffed puppy, which she adamantly called "Diggy".

The room had remained silent for nearly an hour. Although she agreed it was a strange coincidence, Kendra firmly believed Quincy and his pharmacy had nothing to do with April's disappearance. Voices clouded Riley's thoughts.

"Why don't you just go? You should just walk in and look around. What's the harm in that?" Riley clenched her eyes tight, hoping it would make the voices cease, but it only made them louder.

"What if he knows something, Riley? Listen to your gut. Something is wrong here." She sprang from the couch.

"I have to go." She directed at Kendra, walking back toward her bedroom.

"Go?" Kendra quickly followed her down the hallway.

"I'm going to Healix." She whispered, opening her closet. Kendra lunged over Riley and closed the doors.

"Absolutely not. You know he's working today. He can't know you're out." Riley pried Kendra's hand off the door and proceeded to open it again. Kendra slammed it.

"You can't just waltz in. He'll have the cops called immediately. It was his idea to have you arrested in the first place! It's suicide. You're *not* going."

Riley forcefully shoved Kendra's hands off the door again, this time, making her stumble backwards.

"I have to do this, Kendra. I may get nothing out of this, but what do you expect me to do? I'm trying to find your daughter. This is why you bailed me out, ISN'T IT?" Riley screamed. Kendra held her face in her hands.

Riley turned back toward the closet and rifled through her clothes until she found an old hoodie. Kendra, still whimpering, put her damp hand on Riley's shoulder.

"You're…going to need a hat too," Kendra said, collecting herself. Riley pivoted and wrapped her arms around her.

"I'm sorry I made you cry. But I needed you to understand. You have to let me go." Riley unlinked from her hold on Kendra. She grabbed the sunglasses and baseball cap on the nightstand. She stuffed her hair into the back of the hat to form a ponytail. She shimmied uncomfortably, knowing this was a style she would never wear.

"I'm scared, terrified even. But so is April." Riley stormed back through the hallway and into the living room with purpose. She grabbed the receipt from the table and placed it in her front hoodie pocket. "Stay here," Riley called out to Kendra.

"Just try not to run into him, okay?" Kendra begged.

"I won't be long," Riley reassured her after a short pause.

———

Riley walked out the front door and didn't look back. She followed her driveway down to the sidewalk. The pharmacy was only a few blocks away, and Riley needed the fresh air to clear the horrible thoughts in her head.

Flowering trees lined the street, sending a sweet fragrance throughout the town. She walked swiftly and checked her phone to make sure she was going the right way.

"*Take a right, a left, and another right,*" she said to herself. The quick eight-minute walk swiftly turned into five, then three, then one, until she rounded the corner and saw the giant red Healix logo staring back at her.

The windows were filled with promotions of discounted beauty products, buy-one-get-one snacks, and information about seasonal allergies.

Riley put on her sunglasses as her last defense in concealing her identity before calmly opening the door. A bell chimed as she walked in, alerting everyone of her presence. Her heart palpitated at the thought of being in the same space as Quincy.

She looked around cautiously. A woman was sniffing different shampoo bottles, while a worker was restocking drinks on the opposite side of the store. She walked down the aisle directly in front of her to avoid being in plain sight. She observed the vitamins and supplements, pretending to be interested in a bottle of magnesium.

"What am I doing here? This is pointless. I should just go," she thought to herself, carefully placing the bottle back where she found it. She walked down the rest of the aisle and turned the corner to another. She immediately stopped. Her feet were glued to the floor, and her mind was instantly transported back to the night April disappeared.

This out-of-body experience was triggered by a smell, a specific floral scent...but where was it coming from? Riley snapped back and was determined to track it down. She searched the aisle high and low for what could be emitting the smell until she reached the auto care section. There, at eye level, were the car vent clips and air fresheners.

Her nostrils flared, searching for the scent like a bloodhound. Her hands must have rifled through more than twenty different packages before finally finding the last one remaining - *Hibiscus Tiki, A Healix Exclusive.*

The package was cracked slightly. Her fingers grazed the broken plastic before bringing it closer to her nose. Riley's eyes squinted with contempt. That was it. The same air freshener from the car that took April. This discovery didn't bring Riley any closer to actually finding April, but it did give her a comforting sense of familiarity. She felt like she was on the right track.

Riley knew the air freshener had to come with her. With tingling fingers, she confidently took it up to the check-out desk, which was at the pharmacy counter.

Her steps shook the whole building. Everyone in the store was staring daggers at her. Riley kept her focus straight ahead. She approached the cashier, who was on his phone, unaware of her presence. He was a younger, teenage boy with greasy brown hair. Polka-dotted pimples covered his cheeks, and he wore a dingy white polo with the company logo on the left of his chest.

Riley carefully placed the air freshener on the counter, hoping to capture the attention of the boy.

"Hey John!" A voice called from the back of the pharmacy. The boy immediately turned to look. "You need to go on break. I'll cover you for the next fifteen," the man in the back said.

"Aight," the boy called, nonchalantly. He looked at Riley just before walking away. "Hey boss, you got a customer," the boy yelled back into the void. He faced Riley again. "Someone will be right with you, ma'am."

Riley nodded and observed all of the medication bottles behind the counter. Cough syrups, allergy meds, and nasal sprays lined the shelves; a true sign that spring was in full effect. Just as she was comparing the differences between them all, a man moved into her view, and a chill ran down her back through her legs.

He was a taller man in a white lab coat. Riley's eyes slowly moved up the man's torso until she saw his clear, deep complexion.

A salt and pepper goatee covered his chin. Thin wire-frame glasses sat on the bridge of his nose. His eyes were reminiscent of pools of algae. At last, standing before Riley was April's father, Quincy. The real Quincy.

"Hi, ma'am. Was this all today?" Quincy said, picking up the air freshener and trying to make eye contact through Riley's sunglasses. She managed to squeeze out the faintest "mhm" before diverting her attention to pull out a five-dollar bill from her pocket. Though she had never met him, his voice sounded strangely familiar.

"Have you used this one before? Oh, you'll love it. It's my favorite, and you can only get it here!" He held it closer to his nose and took a whiff. "Hm, this one is already open. Did you want to go grab a different one?"

"Mm, no." Riley squeaked.

"Well, alright then," Quincy replied, happily tossing it into a plastic bag. Riley's heart turned to ice, then exploded into a million pieces.

"Please stop talking. Please hurry up."

"STOP TALKING."

"HURRY UP!" Riley said in her head repeatedly. She smiled to conceal her discomfort.

"That will be $3.19, please," Quincy said. She handed the bill to him, and their fingers grazed one another. Riley's stomach flipped upside down.

108

She tried her best to look through him as he counted her change. Behind him, in plain sight, was a gray hoodie folded over the desk chair. The sleeve hung down over the side and showed a red embroidered "H". In any other circumstance, such a mundane detail wouldn't flash on Riley's mental radar, but this wasn't just any hoodie. It was the same hoodie peppered with raindrops on the night April went missing. All of the pieces were falling into place. The smell, the voice, the clothes…the man.

Riley's throat constricted with the tension in the air. Her legs burned with pins and needles. Her feet turned numb, nearly unable to hold the weight of her body for much longer. Her fragmented leads and minutiae details lead her to one conclusion, Quincy knows where April is, or at the very least, where she went that night.

"Um, ma'am?" She heard faintly. Riley's vision refocuses. "Here's your change. Is everything …alright? You zoned out for a moment there." Quincy questioned, holding out the leftover bill and coins.

"I'm fine, thank you," Riley said chillingly, trying her best to conceal her real voice.

"Oh, okay, well…Thanks for stopping in. Have a great rest of your day!" Quincy said warmly. Riley was already halfway out of the store.

She pushed on the door, but it was locked shut. Riley nearly slammed into the glass and repeatedly tried opening the door with no success. Looking at the door confused, the worker stocking drinks called out. "Other door, ma'am." Riley switched her grip to the other door, and the bell chimed just as it did when she arrived.

She frantically ran around the side of the building and immediately fell to her knees. Confusion, disgust, and pure shock consumed every inch of her body. Through her manic state, her brain managed to guide her.

"Pull yourself together, Riley. Get up and run home to tell Kendra." Energy surged through Riley's veins. She picked herself up and darted back to her house.

——

Riley sprinted home without stopping or taking a breath. She busted through the door and found Kendra sitting on the couch playing a game on her phone. Riley's cheeks were rosy with windburn and stained with mascara-soaked tears.

She ripped her sunglasses off her face in anger and threw them on the floor. She released the pharmacy bag from her grip and shook out her annoyingly tight ponytail.

Kendra stood up and crossed her arms.

"Did he see you?" Kendra asked concerningly. Riley, annoyed by this being her first and only question, responded sarcastically.

"Not only did he see me, but he talked to me."

Kendra's jaw dropped. "But…did he know it was you? He had to have known. Oh my God, what are we going to do?!"

Riley watched Kendra spiral.

"You need to go into hiding. Yeah, that's it. He can't do anything if he doesn't know where you are! Maybe a hotel for a few days, or until your trial. The Hampton just opened down the street! Yes! That's good! Or maybe…"

"It was him," Riley said calmly. Her body remained stiff except for the tips of her fingers, which uncontrollably twitched.

Kendra kept babbling. "Maybe I can call my mom, and you can live in her basement for a while. Quincy never willingly goes over there." Kendra continued frantically, pacing in circles around the living room.

"It was…him," Riley said, louder. The twitching in her fingers moved up to her wrists. She gripped her skin tightly, trying not to explode.

Still, no response from Kendra.

"No, no, I couldn't do that to her. She is awful about keeping secrets. Oh, I know! We could go-"

"IT WAS HIM," Riley screamed at the top of her lungs, louder than her voice had ever been before. Her hands released from her wrists, and her arms flung out in front of her. She took a deep breath, and her veins pulsated in her head.

"What…was…him? Who is him?" Kendra asked, startled by Riley's explosion of emotion. Riley walked over to Kendra and placed her hands on her shoulders, then slowly lowered her to the floor. Riley's nervous energy flowed through her arms and into Kendra.

"I don't know how, and I don't know why, but Quincy took April. It was him I saw in the car that night. He's The Man in Gray."

"But…but…he was working late that night. He told me he was working late that night!"

Realization set in, and the light drained from Kendra's eyes. She projectile-vomited all over the floor. Riley quickly moved to the side and held Kendra's hair back, rubbing gently between her shoulder blades. She collapsed, covered in her own spew, still being held by Riley. Her gaze faded into an unresponsive haze. After minutes of lying nearly unconscious, she made a slight twitch. She faintly grabbed Riley's wrists and muttered, "How do you know…?"

———

Riley spent the next fifteen minutes sitting on the floor, wiping the vomit from Kendra's hair and replaying her experience at the pharmacy. She paused only to console Kendra as she wept.

"I just don't understand," Kendra said during her outbursts. "Why would he take his own daughter? Why would he hide our daughter from me?" Riley sat in silence and utter confusion, unable to answer her questions.

"Why would Quincy facilitate this elaborate plan to take his own daughter? Where was he hiding her?" Riley thought. She looked up at Kendra, who had suddenly stopped crying and was staring at the door behind Riley. She calmly whispered, "I don't understand. But I'm about to." Kendra stood up and marched toward the door.

"Wait! Where are you going?" She questioned, pulling on Kendra's arm to stop. Kendra whipped back toward Riley.

"*We,*" Kendra started, "are going back to my house to wait for him. He gets home in an hour."

Kendra turned back toward the door and slipped on her shoes. She motioned for Riley to follow, but she was paralyzed. Kendra went from frantically devising a plan to hide her for the foreseeable future to bringing her right into Quincy's home.

"Uh…are you sure you want to…"

Rage ignited in Kendra's eyes. "Riley, I trust you. If you said he is the one who took my daughter, nothing is going to stop me from confronting him TODAY." Kendra yelled. Riley's eyes grew as wide as a full moon. All she could do was slowly nod her head. She quickly grabbed the bag from the pharmacy and darted out the door after Kendra.

As they approached Kendra and Quincy's home, Riley's head was filled with emotional memories. This was the first time she had been to the house since April disappeared. She asked herself if she was ready to see all of April's toys in the playroom or her favorite blanket in her crib. More questions she didn't have answers to.

While Riley wrestled with her emotions, Kendra wasted no time exiting the car. The driver's side door slammed, shaking Riley's seat. Kendra ran up the driveway.

Riley slowly unbuckled, taking deep, calming breaths with every movement. She followed Kendra up the driveway and into their empty garage.

As they stepped into the house, she expected to be greeted by a disheveled mess. To her surprise, every room was spotless. Everyone handles grief and pain differently, but Riley couldn't help feeling a bit silly that the three-week-old popcorn was still on her living room floor.

She walked through the hallway and laid the plastic pharmacy bag on the dining room table.

She passed by the playroom, which thankfully had the door shut. Kendra sat down at the table, hands placed firmly in front of her body. Her fingers tapped to an unknown beat. Riley stood still.

"Uh, what are you doing?" Riley questioned.

"I'm waiting." Kendra retorted quickly.

"You're going to just sit here and wait until he comes home?"

"Mhmm." Kendra said, mocking Riley.

"Is…it okay if I grab a drink?" Kendra nodded, silently shooing her away. Her eyes were locked on the door.

As she entered the kitchen, her shoes faintly slipped on the freshly polished tile floor. She opened the stainless steel fridge and was blinded by the light reflecting off the cans of cola on the top shelf.

Rows of peach Fact-Tea and sparkling water filled the bottom shelves. Just in case Kendra wanted one, she reached for two Fact-Teas and shut the door. She quickly took a sip of her drink, carelessly dribbling tea out of the sides of her mouth and down the bottle. She wiped her face with her sleeve and approached the dining room again.

Drips lingering on the outside of the bottle created trail-like breadcrumbs through the house. Riley put the extra drink in front of Kendra, though she didn't budge. With a slight scowl on her face, Kendra was a gargoyle. Though made of stone, she could pounce at any moment.

Riley sat a few spots down from her at the table. The crack of her bottle opening rang through the dining room.

She flipped the lid to reveal her Fact-Tea Fact, which read, "#727 - A spider's silk is stronger than steel."

"*Hmm…*" Riley thought.

"You know," Riley said to Kendra, "I don't know how much I believe these Fact-Tea facts. Some of them seem a bit wacky. Like this one says, 'A spider's silk is stronger than steel'…I don't see companies employing spiders to build skyscrapers, you know?" Riley joked, trying to lighten the mood. Still, nothing from Kendra.

Riley's smile faded, and she mentally noted to remove that joke from her stand-up routine.

With a heavy sigh, Riley pressed her forehead to the table. The subtle smell emitting from the handmade cherry wood dining table was oddly soothing. It reminded her of chopping wood with her grandfather, Ken. In his youth, he owned a tree removal company called *"The Arbor Barber,"* which Riley always thought was clever. Every summer, she would spend weeks working with him and his crew. She would find wood chips in her hair and shoes for weeks after her time with them, though they never bothered her one bit...

———

The front door closed abruptly. "Hey, hon, how was your-" The voice paused. "Oh, I didn't know you were inviting company over?"

Riley sprang from her stupor. Her head was indented from resting against the table.

The lights were dim, as night was quickly approaching. Grogginess turned to confusion, which morphed into fear as she regained her vision.

Kendra sat in the same spot, and Quincy ominously filled the doorway. Angered by her presence, Quincy exploded.

"How did you get out of jail? And into my house? Kendra? What is this?!" Quincy demanded. Kendra didn't say a word. She slowly rose from her chair; eyes locked on Quincy. Her hands grazed the dining room table and caressed the plastic bag. Riley and Quincy glanced at one another, confused, before turning their attention back to Kendra. She slowly pulled the broken air freshener from the bag and held it out in front of his face. Quincy didn't move.

"Can someone tell me what's happening right now?" Quincy walked further into the dining room.

"I know it was you," Kendra said softly.

Quincy took the air freshener forcefully from her hand.

"You know WHAT was me? Stop playing games and tell me what the hell is going on." Quincy's voice started to quiver with each word he spoke.

The temperature in the room skyrocketed. He laid the air freshener back on the table and saw a glimpse of the receipt in the bag. He shook it free from the plastic and, after examining it, looked straight at Riley.

"That was you? At Healix today!?" He pointed. He slammed his wallet and keys on the table. Riley jumped from her chair and backed away. "Get the hell out of my house before I call the police and take you back to where you belong. How dare you show your face here?" he said, pulling his phone from his pocket.

Fire festered in Riley's body. Playing dumb was one thing, but deliberately trying to ruin her life for a crime he knew she didn't commit was another. The level of carelessness with the fate of her existence sent her over the edge. This was her chance, and she wasn't about to blow it.

"Oh, cut it, Quincy." Riley's lips had a mind of their own. Quincy and Kendra stood motionless.

"You know, I had plenty of time to think while I was locked away in a concrete box, awaiting my fate, cold…tired…and terrified. Being absolutely pulverized by the inmates who all thought I had made your little girl disappear. The girl who I looked after like she was my own daughter, while you were off working or doing God knows what. I thought about how absent you were for the last 4 months of your daughter's life, so much so that you couldn't even meet me face to face."

Riley inched closer to Quincy. "But you know what replayed in my head the most? The interaction I had with the man who took your daughter. How stiff and unapproachable he was, with a voice that made the hairs on your arms stand up straight. April's reaction when she realized she was being taken away from me. The smell that sank deep into the seats and floated through the air."

Now just centimeters from him, Riley paused, letting his guilt build for a moment longer.

"The hoodie he was wearing. The shadows that darkened his face. The car he was driving. The rain that poured down my neck and back as he sped away, running over my shoe. And the look on your wife's face when she found out I had made the worst mistake of my entire life." Riley began to whisper. "Or so I thought."

She turned and started walking away from Quincy. "You developed an entire elaborate scheme and framed. Your decision sent the entire town into a frenzy and sent me to jail."

Riley stopped and turned back toward him. "But even after all that time with my thoughts, I still couldn't figure out the final piece of the puzzle."

"Why you did it." Kendra interjected, her voice trembling, and her eyes swelling with tears. "WHERE IS MY DAUGHTER!" Kendra screamed, slamming her hands on the table. Quincy stood stiff, like petrified driftwood stuck in the sand.

Without saying a word, he turned around, locked the deadbolt on the front door, and closed the sunshade on the front window. Kendra and Riley quickly glanced toward one another in fear, unsure of what to do next. Riley took a few steps back while he wasn't looking. She grabbed her Fact-Tea bottle, just in case she needed something to throw.

Quincy turned back toward the girls with hatred in his eyes. Though Riley was trying her best to control her breathing, the thickness of the air was suffocating her.

"SAY SOMETHING!" Kendra screamed.

Quincy inhaled deeply and placed his hands on top of the dining room chair for balance. "My dear," he said ominously. "I'm afraid you're missing a key point in your story."

"Oh yeah? And what's that?" Riley questioned. Quincy turned to look at his wife.

"Kendra, would you like to tell her, or should I?"

the secret

Riley lowered herself onto the dining room chair, gripping the edges of the seat as she braced her weight. The pressure of Quincy's words felt like a hydraulic press collapsing her chest. He loomed above her, collecting the darkness surrounding him as the sun began to set through the windows. Her pupils bounced between him and Kendra, their expressions ping-ponging between betrayal and suspense.

"Tell me what?" Riley demanded, uncomfortably adjusting her posture. Neither of the Fellowes spoke. Kendra scowled at Quincy once more before turning to Riley.

"Ry, don't listen to anything he says. He's the one who took April, remember? We can't trust him!" Kendra pleaded.

Riley, now more confused, looked back at Quincy. "Tell. Me. What." Frustration brewed in the pit of her stomach.

Riley's unease grew as she watched the rapid rise and fall of Quincy's chest. He inched closer to her before sitting down in the seat next to her. She squirmed in her seat as he laid his hand on her thigh. He flashed a smirk before speaking softly.

"Riley, you're a bright, young girl. Have you ever heard of the phrase, '*The end justifies the means*'? It's a paraphrase from Machiavelli."

"Yes. I just don't personally agree with it." Riley said, annoyed, shooing his hand from her lap before crossing her arms.

"Here nor there." Quincy scoffed. "My wife intertwined that philosophy into our lives last year." He angrily looked at Kendra.

"Quincy, you're babbling like always. You don't know what you're talking about," Kendra interrupted. Quincy scooted closer to Riley, softly grabbed her jaw, and forced her to look into his eyes. His touch petrified her.

"I'm not sure how to put this delicately, but April is not our daughter," he stated bluntly, releasing his grip from Riley's face.

"He's lying. He's lying, Riley. HE'S LYING!" Kendra erupted from her seat and screamed at the top of her lungs. Someone had just cut the wrong wire on a ticking time bomb. Riley sat and processed the news as Kendra's mental state started to collapse like a burning building. During the breaks of moaning and screaming, Quincy managed to continue his story.

"There was nothing we wanted more than to build our family. Neither of us grew up in large households, and we knew surrounding ourselves with children of our own would fill that void. Though against our best efforts, we struggled with infertility for the past five years of our marriage. We changed our lifestyles, saw every fertility doctor in Chicago, and even painstakingly tried IVF, yet nothing stuck. We were met with miscarriage after miscarriage until we hit our breaking point." Quincy started.

Kendra had moved to the living room, pacing back and forth while muttering "he's lying" under her breath. Riley's anxiety grew, but she weakly focused her attention back on Quincy.

"After we were at peace with not having a child of our own, we explored the idea of adoption. Yet every agency we spoke to said we weren't ideal candidates." This perplexed Riley. They had the money; they had the house, and they were mentally sound. Kendra began to cough, unable to catch her breath from sobbing profusely.

"Why…didn't they want you?" Riley questioned.

"Well, because of my age and how much I traveled for work," Quincy said shamefully.

"That's it? That seems a bit ridiculous." Riley paused, realizing she was investing too much empathy into this monstrous situation.

"We thought so too, and it destroyed us. Our marriage turned sour. Kendra placed much of the blame on me. But after weeks of mourning the loss of what could have been, we began to settle into our new reality."

Riley's jaw hung limp, whispers of questions disintegrating before reaching her lips. Quincy held up one finger, stopping her before she could break the raw silence. Stunned, her gaze flickered between Quincy and his sobbing wife. Kendra's face was devoid of pigment, as if the truth had sucked the life out of her.

"Or, at least…I did," Quincy said, looking over to Kendra. She had moved from pacing to being huddled in a ball of tears on the couch.

"Oh?" Riley questioned, now emotionless.

"You see, back in August, Kendra had come to the pharmacy to have lunch with me like she did every Wednesday. We usually closed the store for lunch, but I guess I had forgotten to lock the front door that day. In walked a young mother and her daughter. I'll never forget Kendra's expression when they came in." Quincy paused.

"The look of awe quickly morphed into envy, then disappointment, as she watched them interact with each other. The daughter was curious about every item on the shelves, and her mom did her best to explain them all as they made their way up to the pharmacy counter. As they got closer, Kendra was enamored by how much the girl looked like the perfect blend of her and I."

"Because she was meant to be ours," Kendra said before resuming her loud sobs on the couch.

"She was right about that," Quincy said, admittingly. "All of her attributes seemed to match ours perfectly. The mom came in asking to refill her prescription. She told me her normal pharmacy couldn't fill it, and they recommended she try ours. I took the script and told her it would take about ten minutes if she wanted to wait. She agreed, and she and her daughter sat on a bench near the counter. The entire time I was filling the prescription, Kendra's eyes were locked on the girl. Dissecting her voice, her mannerisms, her features. She became obsessed. I didn't realize that this small encounter would change our lives forever."

Quincy stumbled back into one of the dining room chairs. His legs bounced with frustration. He took a deep breath before looking into Riley's eyes as he spoke again.

"Every minute, hour, day that went by, she thought of the girl. She even went so far as to hack into my pharmacy records to find the girl's address. Kendra would go out of her way to run errands in their town in hopes of running into them. What could have been a harmless coincidence turned into forced interactions. She started taking walks around their neighborhood and casually greeted them as she passed their yard." Quincy stopped to collect his thoughts again.

Riley's body felt frail, and her stomach churned with disgust and confusion. She snuck small glances towards Kendra as Quincy continued the story.

"Then, one day, she went too far," Quincy said, choking on his words. Kendra buried her head in her legs in disbelief at what she had done.

"Kendra was walking around the neighborhood when she passed by the girl's house and noticed her playing outside...alone." Riley's eyes widened. Her head snapped toward Kendra's direction.

"You didn't," Riley said, shocked.

"You don't understand!" Kendra screamed. "I knew that girl was meant to be mine." She resumed sobbing and twisting her hair. Quincy retook control of the conversation.

"She went right into that girl's yard and grabbed her without anyone seeing." Quincy chimed in. "She covered her mouth so she wouldn't scream and drove her straight home, dragging her from the life she once knew into a completely new one. She held her squirming body in the front seat and swerved down back roads and side streets to avoid attention." Quincy stood up and walked around the other side of the dining room table. "I was away on business that week. I had no idea what awful crime my wife of eleven years had just committed. Jeopardizing our lives, everything we worked for."

Kendra sat motionless on the couch.

"I came back to my house, and it looked like a daycare. Brand-new toys, games, and stuffed animals covered the floor. My guest room had turned pink, filled with a hand-assembled crib, rocker, and changing table. Painted letters on the wall spelling out A-P-R-I-L, the name we picked if we ever had a baby. I slowly walked into the kitchen to see my wife making dinner, and a highchair in the center of the floor. 'Welcome home, Daddy!' Kendra said to me as I stood frozen in the doorway. The child poked her head around the chair, and that's when I realized what she had done." Quincy said, walking away from the room to catch his breath.

Riley sat alone in silence and stared blankly at the wall in front of her, trying to process what Quincy divulged to her.

Through her peripheral vision, she could see Kendra gazing at her ominously. She slowly turned her head to look at her. Kendra's face was puffy, and her eyes pulsated with blood-filled veins. She frantically pleaded with Riley.

"You have to understand; I didn't mean to hurt anybody. I knew I could give April a good life, a way better life than she had! I was meant to be a mom…HER MOM!" She yelled.

"What is her real name?" Riley snapped back, ignoring Kendra's desperation.

Kendra's face went cold. "April," She condescended. "Her name is April."

Riley's brain wanted to unleash an entire dictionary's worth of words on Kendra, but her lips refused to part. All she could do was cry. Cry for Kendra, who was clearly mentally sick. Cry for the mother who was missing her child. Cry for Quincy, who never wanted to be a part of any of this. And cry for herself, because she was now forcefully twisted into this crime. Quincy waltzed back into the room with a seemingly relaxed demeanor.

"For the first few days, I begged Kendra to take the girl home and do the right thing. The girl was irritable, confused, and noticeably scared. But Riley…my wife… was finally vibrant again. She had a purpose. She had everything she always wanted. She was glowing. Who was I to take that away from her?" Quincy said, fighting with himself.

128

"So, I caved, and we decided to become a family. Spinning a web of lies to shield ourselves from reality. We cut and dyed her hair to change her appearance, and did everything we could to make April comfortable with us. She warmed up to us quicker than we expected. Her past life faded into a distant memory. I took leave from work so we could spend every moment together. After a few weeks, we told our friends and family that we were fostering her, in hopes of being able to adopt her one day. We took family pictures to plaster all over our walls, we took day trips to the library, and for the first time ever, we felt whole. And thus, my dear, the end justifies the means."

Kendra looked at Quincy lovingly for the first time that night, appreciating his sick, twisted words.

"So, where is April now?" Riley blurted, clearly dampening their moment.

Kendra's expression turned sour again, eagerly awaiting Quincy's answer. "The high of being a family quickly wore off for me. I lay awake every night in agony at the choices we made." Quincy retorted. Kendra got up from the couch and crept into the dining room to listen more closely.

"I started picking up more shifts just to get away from the house. I couldn't stand the sight of either of them. And when Kendra told me about you being so involved in April's life, I knew this charade had gone on long enough. So, over the course of those few short months, I thought of ways I could get April back to her mom."

"I'M HER MOTHER!" Kendra screamed, marching right up to Quincy. He forcefully pushed her shoulder back with no remorse, and she fell to the ground. He turned back to Riley.

"But I knew bringing her back to her mother was dangerous. After all, she saw me in the pharmacy that day. I needed a drop-off location where nobody would know who I was. That's when I searched in the pharmacy database and found April's father."

Kendra began to scream. "HOW COULD YOU? YOU LOVED HER! SHE WAS YOUR DAUGHTER!"

"I do love her, Kendra. Which is why I had to do the right thing." Quincy said sternly. "Unfortunately for you, Riley, you made the perfect scapegoat. All I had to do was bait Kendra into letting me pick April up from your house. It set you up to be the catalyst. This gave me enough time to drop April on her father's doorstep in her car seat without anyone noticing.

Sorry for speeding over your shoe, by the way. April's screaming was incredibly agitating, and I just needed to get out of there."

And there it was.

This was the confession Riley had sought for weeks, the answer she had been conjuring up as she lay awake at night. The dots finally connected, and they still led right back to her being at the center.

Kendra continued to scream and slap her hands on the floor in denial. "NO NO NO NO!" She yelled through her tears. Quincy yelled at Kendra about what she had done and how it ruined both of their lives. He screamed that they'll need to move across the country to start over and leave absolutely no trace of what had happened in Clarendon Hills. They argued aggressively, and all Riley could do was witness the eruption. Her mind raced to her next move.

Does she scream?

Does she call the police?

Does she pinch her leg to hopefully awake from this horrific nightmare?

In the heat of their argument, Riley felt a flutter of adrenaline. Her brain screamed at her to run. While the Fellowes were distracted, her eyes quickly scanned the room. She remembered that Quincy locked the front door when he came in, so the only option was the garage door. It was just down the hall to her right. She tried her best to blend into the background and wait for Quincy to start yelling again.

"YOU KNOW I DID THE RIGHT THING, KENDRA," he bellowed. During the heat of the sentence, Riley pivoted her feet and bolted down the hallway.

It didn't take long for the couple to see what she was doing. Realization set in, knowing that if Riley escaped, both Quincy and Kendra were heading to jail.

"STOP HER!" Quincy roared, pushing Kendra toward Riley's direction. Both women raced down the hallway. Riley slammed into the door leading to the garage and quickly fiddled with the doorknob to break free from the house. It wouldn't budge. She was trapped like sand in an hourglass that was slowly sinking toward the bottom.

She panicked, looking for another escape, when Kendra lunged, her eyes blazing with madness. Riley braced herself for the impact as a scream rose up and out of her throat. The weight of Kendra was too heavy to bear, and Riley collapsed to the ground, breaking her fall with the side of her head. Her vision blurred just before the entire house plunged into darkness.

the man in the kitchen

Throbbing waves consumed Riley's skull like a tsunami. Her eyes pulsated as she slowly unclasped her eyelids. Her head rested on the cold hardwood floor that was caked in dust. Her body felt limp, and each breath increased pressure on her temples. Her bottom lip was split, and a metallic taste coated Riley's tongue. Pain and panic blended into an anxiety smoothie. Images, blurred and fragmented, flickered through her thoughts. A black-and-white movie played in her mind. Snapshots of Kendra's deranged eyes were burned into her vision.

Disoriented, she forced herself to claw back to reality. The room came into focus. In the corner, a beige and gold lamp illuminated the room, and on the far wall, a window was shielded by a curtain.

"That's my ticket out of here," she thought. Trying to move, she felt something restrict her. With every wiggle, she felt a warm burning sensation on her wrists. They were tied together with a thick nylon rope. She tried feeling around her back pockets for her phone, but it was missing.

She mustered every ounce of energy to sit up, which remained a challenge as her hands were tied behind her back. She hung her head down, hoping the contraction-like throbbing in her head would stop.

She slowly rose to her feet and hobbled over to the window. Dusk had faded into night, and it was difficult to see where she was. But one thing was very clear - she was on the second floor. If she was in this bad of shape from a simple tackle, who knows what could happen from jumping out of a two-story window?

"There has to be another way," she tried convincing herself. She slinked over to the door and turned around to try to grab the handle. Her hands were just shy of being able to reach it. Frustrated, she bent down and nestled the doorknob between her neck and her shoulder.

She wiggled and shimmied the best she could with no luck. While she was pressed against the door, she heard muffled commotion downstairs. Holding her breath, she tried to decipher what was happening.

"I COULDN'T KEEP LIVING LIKE THIS, KENDRA. WHAT DID YOU EXPECT ME TO DO?"

"YOU NEVER LOVED HER. YOU NEVER LOVED ME."

Smaaaaash

Booooom

Stommmmmp

"WAIT. WHERE ARE YOU GOING? KENDRA! STOP!"

Slam

The commotion silenced, and the echo of Kendra's dramatic exit rang in Riley's ears.

She stumbled back from the door and hobbled over to the window. All she could do was watch Kendra peel out of the driveway, leaving black tire marks on the concrete.

Before Riley could theorize where Kendra was going, heavy footsteps thundered up the staircase, and the door splintered open. Quincy filled the doorframe. His face was cold and stern, but his eyes emitted danger. Riley stood frozen, like a deer in headlights. Her concussed brain struggled to process his appearance. Should she run, scream, throw something...throw up? No option seemed logical. Her body radiated with warm vibrations, and sweat dripped from her scalp.

"I know this looks...bad," Quincy started.

"Bad?" Riley questioned condescendingly.

"Okay, really bad. But listen, Riley, you've got to help me. She's about to hurt someone, or herself." His voice dropped to nearly a whisper as he gripped the doorframe.

"Explain to me why the hell I would help you, Quincy. Your wife just tackled me and gave me a concussion. You tied me up and locked me in a room. Not to mention, you dragged me into this mess in the first place. I don't owe you anything," Riley stood her ground.

Each accusation was a strong blow to Quincy's ego. He became stiff, and his expression dropped. "I'm not giving you a choice, Riley. You're coming with me." Quincy marched toward Riley.

He forcefully wrapped his long, slinky fingers around her bicep and pulled her toward the door. Instead of struggling, she hoped that wherever he was taking her, there would be someone who could help get her out of this mess.

Quincy guided Riley down the staircase and out the front door. A small sliver of sunlight illuminated the horizon. The full moon ominously followed Riley as she was forced into the passenger seat of Quincy's car. The same car that carried April away just a few weeks ago. She felt somber as she caught a glimpse of the empty back seat, where her bright pink car seat used to be.

He slammed the door, and she took the short opportunity to look around his car for anything that could be used as a weapon. But before she could pick up the umbrella from the floorboard with her feet, the driver's door flew open, and Quincy flopped onto the seat. He slid the key into the ignition, and lights illuminated the dashboard. Riley noticed the orange gas light remained on as Quincy sped out of the driveway.

"*Maybe he'll stop for gas, and I can make my escape.*" She turned her gaze to the window and watched a sea of green trees fly by.

Rhythmic vibrations of the tires squealing on the asphalt below added to Riley's uneasiness.

Trapped next to the man who orchestrated this nightmare, she squinted her eyes and wished to be anywhere but there. Quincy menacingly oozed purpose. His hands twitched with anxiety, unable to grip the wheel steadily. His trembling fingers bounced between fidgeting with the air conditioning, moving his visor back and forth, and rolling his window up and down. It didn't take much observation to realize Quincy was on edge.

Being unbuckled and unable to brace herself, Riley's weight was supported by the door and the center console with each twist and turn he made. After speeding through a red light, she'd had enough of his recklessness.

"Are you going to tell me where we're going? Are you trying to find a place to dump my body?" Riley's voice was blunt as she evaluated the severity of the situation.

"Do I look like a killer?" He asked, completely avoiding her first question. Slightly concerned, Riley kept pressuring him for information.

"You asked for my help. What good am I going to be if you don't tell me what you need my help for? I think it's a little-"

Quincy slammed on the brakes in the middle of the street. The car came to a complete stop. Riley was instantly thrown forward, and her body smacked against the dashboard. Disoriented and in pain once again, Riley turned to Quincy. "What in the -" she started.

"Listen here," Quincy forced Riley back against the headrest by her throat. "You're going to sit in that seat and shut up until we get where we're going. No more questions. Understood?"

He released his grip from Riley's throat, and the roar of the engine filled the streets. Warm tears raced down her cheeks like streaks of fire. Uncertain of her fate, visions of her life began to fill behind her eyelids.

The future she dreamed for herself faded into oblivion. Morbidly, only one comforting thought clouded her consciousness. If this ride came to a sudden halt, at least she knew she would be with her mom again, chasing meteors across the galaxy and patrolling the stars. She sniffled silently, hoping to avoid Quincy's attention.

An orange light blinking on the dashboard shattered the tension, highlighting Quincy's face in the darkness.

"Of course," he groaned, frustrated. He abruptly turned down a side street lined with uninviting, poorly lit houses and overgrown shrubbery. The road quickly illuminated as he merged onto a busy freeway. Riley shifted her body toward the window, in hopes of making eye contact with a passerby. But with tinted windows and the night sky, nobody would be able to notice her soundless cry for help.

After weaving through traffic, he swerved toward exit fifteen. The road signs showed a gas station just a mile away. The car came to a halt as Quincy caught a red light.

She observed his dismal expression as the neon red hue illuminated his dastardly face. He must have felt the heat from her eyes.

"I'm really not a bad guy, Riley. Kendra turned our lives upside down," he said as his face turned from red to green. The acceleration pushed Riley further into her seat. "I'm just trying to make things right again."

Riley was too timid to speak. Her tongue felt like sandpaper against the roof of her mouth. Each drop of burning saliva scraped against her throat. She sat quietly as they approached the nearly desolate gas station and subtly observed the surroundings as Quincy pulled next to an open pump.

Two empty cars sat on the unlit side of the mini mart. One car was idling on the opposite side of the pumps, and a couple had just walked out of the mart.

"Okay, this is it. Scream. Shout. Make a scene. Wake up from this nightmare for good." Riley recited to herself. Quincy removed the key from the ignition and placed his hand on the door handle.

"Here we go, three...two..." Riley counted down in her head, readying her vocal cords.

Quincy paused before getting out. "I know where April is," he said, unbuckling his seatbelt and opening the door slowly.

"And I'm taking you to her." He lifted his weight from the seat and grabbed the fuel pump, leaving the door wide open.

Riley's muscles, once aching with pain, were now numb with shock. The idea of escaping was inconsequential. Her mind shifted back to April, where this crazy charade began. Hope blossomed in her chest as she watched the gallons flow from the gas pump. She had come too far to give up on her, and if anyone could save April, it was going to be her.

———

Riley and Quincy continued driving in silence for nearly half an hour. She watched the odometer tick with each passing mile. With no GPS and little knowledge about the area, Riley felt like she was in an abyss of darkness with no light in sight. Anxiously awaiting to see what fate hid in the shadows. Roads turned quickly from exurb to suburb, and homes began to outnumber the trees.

Quincy made a sharp turn down a rundown side street that led to the entrance of South Shore Trailer Park. Lit cigarette butts illuminated the faces of those sitting on their porches as Riley and Quincy cruised down Sandstone Avenue. She caught a glimpse of the yellow "no outlet" sign toward the end of the street, yet Quincy continued on.

Thirteen, eleven, nine. Riley counted the house numbers from the mailboxes. The car abruptly halted in front of the last house on the street. The end of the road stopped just short of the tree line surrounding the house.

The driveway was blocked by none other than Kendra's car. Around the right side, one window emitted an orange glow. The rest of the trailer was engulfed in darkness. Quincy kept the car idling, refusing to put it in park. After sitting for a few moments, Riley turned toward him in confusion. His scowling eyes pierced through to her soul.

"Go in and get April," Quincy said bluntly. Riley turned her body toward the house and then back to Quincy.

"Am I supposed to…knock?" Riley asked, confused about his command.

"I don't care what you do as long as you stop Kendra. She'll listen to you," he said calmly. "Just go and stop her before it's too late." Quincy's expression was stone-cold. "Bring her straight back here."

"*Before it's too late? Late for what?*" Riley asked herself.

Quincy opened the center console of his car and unveiled a small red and black pocketknife. He slowly unlatched the blade and leaned toward Riley. She recoiled and instinctively muttered, "What…what are you doing!?"

Without saying a word, Quincy pushed her left shoulder toward the door, exposing her back to him.

Riley clamped her eyes shut, trying her best to prepare herself for the pain Quincy was about to unleash. He lowered the knife and made contact with the rope confining her wrists.

He sawed the blade against the nylon until it splintered. Relieved, Riley feverishly rubbed her wrists, frowning at the rings of redness and bruising around her arms.

"...Thank you," she said apprehensively. Not only appreciating her newfound freedom, but also the fact that he decided to spare her.

"Go." His voice echoed with bitterness. Quincy unlocked the car doors.

Without hesitation, Riley opened the door and nearly fell from her seat. Stumbling to find her footing, she crept toward the front door into the darkness. After her eyes adjusted, she noticed blades of grass sprouting between the cracks in the concrete as she walked up the steep steps. She gripped the handle of the door but released it quickly. She erringly looked back to see if Quincy was watching her. His eyes, nearly glowing, commanded her to proceed.

"You can do this, Riley. No matter what happens, you know you're going to save April." Riley convinced herself.

After a wealth of courage flooded her veins, she skipped knocking and went straight to open the door. She was ready to make an entrance. After a few jiggles, the door appeared to be locked.

Unsure of her next move, echoes of a familiar voice cascaded through the air. She cautiously backed away from the door and down the steps to swiftly follow the sound of the voice around the side of the house.

She approached the illuminated window with its blinds halfway drawn. Riley wasn't quite tall enough to peek through, so she looked around for something to stand on.

She locked eyes with the fire pit made of bricks in the middle of the yard. Though her wrists were still trembling and raw from the rope, she quickly disassembled the pit to create a makeshift step stool. Finally, she hoisted herself on top of the bricks. Even on her tiptoes, the top of her head just barely reached the bottom of the windowpane, but it was enough for her eyes to look through.

Riley's pupils wandered through what appeared to be the kitchen. Yellowing walls oozed with nicotine stains, and dishes piled high in the sink. She shifted her body to look deeper into the room and saw the edge of Kendra's silhouette and a tall man.

The man was frail and sickly, with bright blonde hair. He was shirtless and covered in faded, blown-out tattoos. Riley scanned his body and noticed he had his hands above his…head.

Her eyes bounced back to Kendra. Riley initially overlooked the cold, metal weapon drawn in her grip. Petrified, she pressed her ear against the house in hopes of hearing what the hell was going on.

"Lady, please - I can help you, but you have to tell me who you are," the man pleaded.

"You don't need to know who I am. Where is my daughter?" Kendra demanded.

"I...I don't know who your daughter is, b-but I can help you find her!" He yelped with a raspy voice, desperately trying anything to get her to lower the weapon. His body was twitching with fear.

"DON'T PLAY DUMB! APRIL, WHERE IS APRIL?"

"I don't know any-" he began. In a bout of psychotic rage, Kendra fired a shot into the ceiling. Riley covered her mouth before letting a shriek escape from her lips. She stumbled back and fell from her pile of bricks. Ears ringing, she quickly got back into position. Bits of drywall had exploded throughout the kitchen. The man had dropped to his knees.

"PLEASE! I'LL DO ANYTHING! I'LL HELP YOU FIND HER!" He screamed, breaking down into a full sob. Kendra was motionless as she absorbed the reaction to her aggressive tactics.

Riley's eyes widened as she understood the scene she was forced into. She stepped back from the window, hoping to catch her breath. With the pit of her stomach on fire, she looked to the woods. The street was barely visible from where she stood, meaning Quincy couldn't see if she made a run for it.

"*I can't do this.*"

Riley flopped on the ground, her back parallel with the earth. Weeds tickled her ears, and she rolled her head from side to side. Clouds shielded the moon and stars and filled the night sky with gloom. She inhaled the evening air and closed her eyes, wishing she were in the comfort of her own home. Her vision was clouded by images of April, but not as she was, what she could be.

Her first day of kindergarten.
Her first bike ride.
Her first sleepover.
Her first school dance.

Riley's smile faded to tears. With Kendra's fugue state, it was uncertain whether April would get to experience all of life's beautiful offerings.

"I can do this," she said, standing firmly. This realization was the adrenaline rush she needed. She crept toward the back of the house. The man's whimpers became fainter as she approached the back door. With her fear shadowed by heroic energy, she flew up the steps and pushed the button on the door handle. To her surprise, the door cracked open. She paused, knowing there was no going back after stepping inside.

She opened the door just enough for her body to slink through. The opening revealed a long, dark hallway with an orange light glowing at the end.

She stepped over the threshold and heard Kendra's tirade echo throughout the house. The sound of her deranged voice sent a shiver down her aching spine.

Screams from the kitchen snapped Riley into focus. She frantically searched for a room to hide in, catch her breath, and hopefully find a weapon to defend herself. The wooden floorboard creaked as she darted into the first room to her right. She slowly closed the door and twisted the latch to lock it. She breathed heavily.

"*Okay. Now what?*" She thought, closing her eyes and turning her back toward the door. The room smelled sweetly of lavender, and a cloud-shaped night light softly lit the room. A bin of stuffed animals was piled on the floor.

There was a rocking chair in the corner and a large wooden crib. She stepped carefully toward the crib and peeked over the railing to see a mop of curly hair, pink bunny pajamas, and two bright green eyes staring back at her. Riley stood in utter disbelief.

A soft voice began to coo.

"Ry Ry?"

bang

Riley's lower half turned gelatinous at the sound of the delicate voice. Her knees buckled, and she fell at eye level with the little girl.

"A…April?" Riley questioned in disbelief.

The little girl immediately gripped the crib rails and excitedly jumped up and down.

"RY RY RY RY RY!" The little girl shrieked. Riley sprang from her knees to cover April's mouth.

"Shh, shh. I know you're excited, but we have to be quiet," Riley whispered while choking back tears.

"Ry Ry, shh," April whispered back and held one finger up to her mouth.

She lifted her arms up to Riley, silently begging to be held. A toothy grin formed between April's chubby cheeks. Her eyes blinked delicately, trying to absorb every ounce of Riley's presence standing before her.

Riley leaned into the crib and embraced April for the first time in nearly a month. Their hearts beat against one another in unison. The emptiness in Riley's soul had been filled with genuine relief.

The girl's head nestled into her chest. Tears flowed from Riley's eyes and soiled her pajama shirt. She was entranced by the smell of April's hair and the softness of her skin. The warmth of April's small body radiated brightly, making her worries melt into oblivion.

This rare moment of peace was splintered by a shrill, maniacal voice that threatened to shatter the windows of the trailer.

"I KNOW YOU'RE HIDING HER, TRAVIS. TELL ME WHERE SHE IS." Kendra's voice exploded from the room down the hall. Muted arguments reverberated through the walls. It wouldn't be long before she charged past the man in the kitchen and found her way to April's room.

"We're going to get you out of here," Riley whispered in April's ear. She scanned the room to gather some of her belongings. Though the room was shaded, a familiar shape in the corner of the room caught her eye. She tiptoed to April's diaper bag and began stuffing diapers, wipes, and clothes into it, completely disregarding organization. She added a few stuffed animals, zipped it up, and threw it over her free shoulder.

Insistent on not going back into the door she came through, she looked around for another exit. She hustled over to the window next to the crib. With one hand, she attempted to hoist the window open, but her weak fingers trembled. She sat April down on the floor for a moment, which made her whine.

"Just a second; I need to find a way out of here."

April looked perplexed as Riley thrust her body weight into opening the window. Her hands glided across the edges of the frame, and flakes of paint and rust coated her fingertips. Riley wiped the residue onto her pants with frustration and embraced April once again. The only way out was…the door. Riley took a deep breath, squeezing her body closer to April's.

"Okay, April," Riley whispered, rocking her smoothly from side to side. "We're going to run really, really fast, okay? I need you to hold on tight to me."

"Ya," April replied quickly, unaware of the impending chaos this escape could cause. Riley grabbed the door handle but paused before unlocking it. *"I don't want to run back to Quincy, but I don't have another way of getting out of here,"* she thought to herself. *"Maybe I can find a neighbor who will help me. Yeah, yeah, okay. That'll work."* Riley assured herself confidently. She carefully unlocked the handle and twisted it open. The door creaked slightly as she and April began to slip past.

bang! flash!

THUD.

The paintings on the walls shook loose from their fasteners. Another bullet fled from Kendra's weapon and sent shivers down Riley's spine. April shuddered, thinking the sound was from a thunderstorm, and buried her face in Riley's shoulder. Riley peeked down the hallway, expecting to see drywall bits cover the floor, but was horrified to see a much ghastlier scene. The man in the kitchen was no longer on his knees, begging for peace.

He was prone on the floor.

The tip of his head just passed the threshold of the kitchen and into Riley's sight. Thick blood began to pool around his neck, slowly trickling down the hallway toward the girls.

Riley forced April's head to stay down, shielding her from the murder scene caused by Kendra. Riley mustered the mental strength to run out the door. But the floor had turned to quicksand, entrapping her legs. With weighted ankles, Riley shuffled down the hallway toward the back door. With every step she took, the door faded like a mirage on a hot summer day. Her breathing grew shallow, her lungs aching for oxygen.

"Did I just witness a murder? Is Kendra a murderer?" Riley repeated in her head. *"No, she couldn't be. This...this is all a big misunderstanding."* Just before clinging to the doorknob, the fire throughout her body was extinguished by the sound of footsteps down the hall and the chilling tone of a familiar voice.

"Riley?" Kendra questioned. Riley pivoted. "What are you..." she stuttered, noticing April's body wrapped around her torso. "Oh, Riley! You saved our April. Now...now we can be a happy family again!" Kendra called in a delighted tone. Her once-white shirt was splattered and stained with blotches of remains. The clumps of hair escaping her messy ponytail were erratic. Her dilated pupils filled her irises.

"Bring April to me, Riley. Mommy is here!" Kendra placed the smoking gun in her back pocket and held her cheeks with excitement.

April uncomfortably squirmed at the sound of Kendra's voice. "Mama?" She questioned, speaking into Riley's shirt, trying to peek at Kendra down the hall. Riley kept her hand firmly on the back of April's head so she couldn't see. She squeezed her tighter and slowly backed down the hallway toward the door again.

"Where…where are you going?" Kendra stuttered. Riley's eyes shifted to the man in the kitchen, lying still on the floor behind Kendra's feet. Her body swelled with fear as she reluctantly met Kendra's gaze again.

"What? This?" Kendra pointed at the man. "You don't understand, Riley. He was hurting my April, our April, by keeping her away from us. I did what I had to do to protect her and myself! She belongs with her mother," Kendra said, strangely calm and collected.

For a moment, Riley believed her. It was easier that way. The drama of this sick, twisted night would vanish, and she could go home without blood on her hands. But Riley was never one to take the easy way out.

"You killed that man, Kendra," Riley said, spewing ice shards with each word. Her heart revved like an engine. She delicately touched one of the crooked photos of April and her father on the wall to straighten it.

"You stole April from her family. You and Quincy let me sit in jail while I thought of ways to find someone who was never yours to find!" Riley looked into Kendra's deranged brown eyes. "You lied to me. You've lied to me since I met you! I'm taking April somewhere safe. Away from you, and away from Quincy. You are not her mother."

Kendra's smile immediately dropped into a scowl. "You're wrong, Riley. You're not," Kendra started, raising the gun from her back pocket to eye level, "going anywhere."

"Kendra, p-put that down. You could...hurt April," Riley said.

"Mmm, not to worry. I'm a pretty good shot." Kendra retorted as she cocked the hammer and rested her finger on the trigger.

The women stood across from each other for what felt like an eternity. Riley refused to move, and Kendra wasn't backing down until she had April in her clutches.

"You know, this really is a shame, Riley," Kendra said, tilting her head to the side. "You had such a beautiful life ahead of you. Think about all of the novels you'll never write. How Griddle will starve all alone in that house, without you. You'll never meet your soulmate or have children of your own. Your whole life will end, right here, between the walls of this dingy trailer," Kendra said with a cold smirk. "Unless you give me back my daughter. Then all of this would go away."

154

Riley continued to cradle April's curls, protecting her from her pseudo-mother's cruelty. Her eyes stung as she stared blankly at Kendra, trying to pinpoint her next move. "*Think, Riley, think!*" She screamed to herself. Every thought led to homicide.

"I'm not going to stand here all day, Riley. Start walking toward me, or this bullet is coming straight for your head."
Riley gasped at the thought of April witnessing something so horrifying. She followed Kendra's strict commands and inched closer down the long corridor.

Her shoes scuffed the floor with each step, dragging her weight as much as possible to slow her stride.

"FASTER!" Kendra yelled. April sniffled, terrified of the demonic voice. Fearful of the distance, Riley refused to look ahead and instead watched her steps graze across the floor.

"LOOK AT ME!" Kendra bellowed. Riley slowly lifted her eyes and was startled by a silhouette looming behind Kendra. Dark hands feverishly gripped a neon nylon rope. Riley's body twitched, and she immediately retreated backward toward the door.

"WHAT ARE YOU DOING? GIVE ME MY BABY BACK! I'M GOING TO-" The figure emerged from the shadows to reveal his face. He gripped the rope tightly with both hands and wrapped it firmly around Kendra's neck. Though stunned, she instinctively dropped her weapon and grabbed the rope, desperate for relief. Riley watched in agony as the man who tried to ruin her life just a few short weeks ago was now here to save it.

"GO RILEY! TAKE APRIL AND RUN!" Quincy screamed and pulled back on the rope tighter. Kendra's face morphed into shades of red and purple. Riley backed away as the sounds of Kendra's anguish rang in her ears. She turned toward the door, and her stride evolved into a hundred-yard sprint.

She busted through the screen door and completely missed all three concrete steps that led to the backyard. Stumbling onto the grass, she gripped April's body as if her life depended on it. She looked back through the door to see Kendra breaking free from Quincy's trap. With April's diaper bag hung over her shoulder, Riley darted through the grass and into the tree line.

She tore through the brush and broken tree limbs like a spooked rabbit running from a fox. Her heart pounded against her chest as her feet slammed against the earth. With the moonlight as her only guide, she ventured deeper into the forest's shadows. The sound of crunching leaves and snapping twigs made Riley's head whip back, fearing that Kendra was riding her tail.

After nearly a half mile of sprinting, she slowed to a light jog, which quickly faded to a brisk walk. She was glistening from the scurry and the overwhelming feeling of trepidation. Her body rested against a thick tree stump, hoping it wasn't doused with sap or spiders. Her eyes faded to a close for a few moments, and she curled her body around April's for support.

April was surprisingly calm. The vibrations of Riley's steps almost lulled her to a slumber. She focused on the rise and fall of her chest, trying to synchronize her heartbeat with April. A voice erupted from the tree line that broke her focus.

"RILEY? COME BACK HERE, RILEY. I KNOW YOU'RE OUT THERE." The sound of Kendra's menacing tone shot a bolt of electricity through her body. She pushed off the tree trunk and ventured further through the forest.

"RUN RILEY! RUN!" Quincy shouted. His voice faded as she weaved through the trees.

bang! bang!

The sound of gunfire echoed through the leaves as sleeping birds fled their nests. Gripping her chest, her hand could feel her heart racing. Another life, lost? Riley wondered. She was determined not to be the next victim in Kendra's bloodbath. Her shoes pounded the ground as the joints in her knees sizzled. The weight of April's body was wearing on every muscle. She needed to rest soon before her body gave out entirely.

Her feet stopped just short of a river. The moon's beams illuminated the small ripples. On the other side of the water, she saw glimpses of a city through the trees.

"That's where I need to go," Riley whispered to herself. She took a deep breath and hoisted April's now-limp body up higher on her shoulder. The tip of her sneaker collided with the top of the river. The mesh on the tip of her shoe soaked up the water like a sponge. Her skin puckered with goosebumps. She pulled back for just a moment before plunging her entire foot.

With the darkness concealing how deep the water was or what may be lurking beneath, Riley meticulously placed each step. The water swirled gracefully and slowly crept up her body as she reached the middle of the river. The water tickled the bottom of April's feet, making her squirm in Riley's arms.

"Just a little further," Riley whispered in April's ear. The calming tone of her voice settled her to sleep.

She fought through the resistance of the water and slowly ventured to the other side. Her clothes were sopping wet as she tiptoed along the riverbank. She crumbled to the ground, still clinging to April. The diaper bag rolled off her shoulder, and she lay her head on top like it was a pillow. Rocks and dirt clung to her skin like glue. Her hair was twisted into knots, and a crawling sensation prickled up and down her legs. Though uncomfortable, Riley sat still. She was too weak to move. The only part of her functioning was her mind. The sound of Kendra's gunfire mixed with Quincy's shriek as he strangled her haunted every thought. Her brain had started to settle, just when April sat straight up from Riley's chest.

"Dada?" April said, disoriented, completely out of the blue. She wiped her eyes, hoping to take in more light, but was overcome with darkness. Images of the man in the kitchen flashed in Riley's view. His once blonde hair turned crimson. Riley sat up and gripped April tightly.

"I'm here, baby. It's okay."

As she held April's warm body, she was transported back to when she used to care for her in the evenings. Though normally a fantastic sleeper, April would try to fight it every once in a while. Riley would walk her around the kitchen and the living room, singing "All My Loving" by the Beatles. The sound of Riley's singing was like a sleeping potion.

"Close your eyes, and I'll kiss you," Riley sang softly. April settled back into her arms.

"Tomorrow, I'll miss you. Remember, I'll always be true…" Riley's eyes stung. She tried her best to finish the song while blubbering.

"Everything will turn out okay, April. I promise." She whispered to her as she stroked her hair away from her face. April's breathing slowed, and her body weight melted once again.

"*Phew*," Riley thought to herself. Reminiscent sweat and river water left a film over her entire body. She carefully removed April from her chest and laid her on the ground for a moment. Riley opened the diaper bag and pulled out a blanket to set out for April.

After transferring her to a cozier spot, Riley looked deeper in the bag for a towel, wipes…anything to remove the grime from her skin. Riley quickly changed April's diaper, as it couldn't hold any more liquid. She then found a few loose granola bars, which Riley was sure would be helpful later, a half-full bottle of water, spare clothes, a few diapers, and…a pill bottle buried at the bottom.

She paused from her search to examine it. Though her eyes had adjusted to the darkness, she still had difficulty reading the prescription. The label was tattered and worn, but the date on the bottle showed it was prescribed in August of last year. She smoothed out the label to reveal it was a medication called Lithium.

"Uh, like the battery?" Riley questioned curiously.

The corner of the sticker exposing the patient's name was too distorted to decipher in the dark.

"Must have been her dad's. Hmm. Whatever." Riley shrugged, throwing the bottle back into the bag. She grabbed a small burp cloth from a side pocket and began scrubbing her face. Her eyes pulsed from the pressure and the salt in her sweat. She stood up and squeezed the remaining moisture from her clothes before lying back down beside April to close her eyes.

———

Riley awoke violently, confusing the sound of a nearby tree branch for gunfire. She observed her surroundings, terrified she was going to find Kendra standing over them with a pistol in their faces. She placed her hand on her chest to slow her rapid, shallow breaths.

After orienting herself back to reality, Riley watched April as she dreamt. She hoped happier thoughts would enchant her. Maybe she was playing with her toys on a cloud made of cotton candy or splashing in the world's largest ball pit.

April's hands twitched as Riley's fingers tickled them. She had since turned over on her belly and soothed herself by sucking her thumb. Riley rubbed her back, wiping away rogue dirt from her makeshift bed.

She cradled April in a blanket cocoon before standing up from their camping spot. She walked up a small hill just a few feet away to get a better view of the city. She looked back every few moments to ensure April didn't wake up frightened or roll toward the river. With no phone and no watch, Riley grew disoriented, staring at the distant lights through the trees, wondering how late it really was. Through the branches, she saw that the moon was approaching the horizon line.

"How long was I asleep for? Longer than I thought..." Riley realized. "I have to keep moving." She said, walking back down the hill to April.

She slung the diaper bag over one shoulder and laid April's limp body over the other. She moaned ever so slightly before snuggling back into Riley's grip.

Riley looked out across the river, silently counting the endless ripples from fish swimming below. Inhaling the chilled air deep into her lungs, she knew this night was far from over. Her tongue grazed across her brittle, purple lips to moisten them.

Each gust of wind stiffened her damp clothing, causing her teeth to chatter. All ten toes gripped her wet shoes as she struggled to walk up the hill once again. However, she didn't mind being uncomfortable. With newfound fire in her eyes, she pushed forward with determination to put an end to her never-ending nightmare.

Stack of hotcakes

Riley stomped through mud, twigs, and vines for what felt like hours before reaching the city line, all while supporting the weight of April's sleeping body. The sun had begun to peek over the horizon. The last memories of the night clung to the sky.

Miraculously, they'd made it through the night without Kendra finding them. Riley's lips were chapped and cracked as her dry tongue rubbed against them. Her last drink was the Fact-Tea she took from Kendra and Quincy's fridge before the confrontation. A metallic taste lingered in her mouth. She craved the relief of sustenance.

With only a few sips of water and a granola bar in the diaper bag, Riley chose to save them for April. Nervousness nestled in her mind. With no access to her bank account or any cash on hand, she wasn't sure where their next meal was going to come from.

Riley exited the tree line and sighed a large breath of relief. The forest they were hiding in paralleled a small, desolate town. She stepped onto the concrete sidewalk, her damp sneakers squishing with each step. As she walked along the pathway next to the street, her knees threatened to buckle.

Quickly looking for a place to collect herself, she noticed a metal bench on the opposite side of the street.

They made a quick dash across the cobblestone road without looking either way. She slumped down on the bench, jolting April awake.

"Well, good morning, sunshine!" Riley exclaimed, fighting through her exhaustion to stretch her face into a smile. April smiled brightly while rubbing her eyes.

"Waa waa," April demanded.

"You want some water? No problem." Riley dug through the diaper bag to pull out the half-full plastic bottle. She awkwardly held the bottle up to April's mouth. She was used to a sippy cup, but she managed to let only a few dribbles escape from her lips.

"Tank yew," April bubbled, wiping her mouth with her bare arm. Riley eyed the bottle before reluctantly taking a small sip. She wanted to preserve as much as possible.

After another quick diaper change, Riley sat April on the bench next to her. She poked her fingers through the small holes and examined every scratch in the metal.

Riley looked up from April to observe the town. With streetlamps as her only source of light, she admired the architecture of the brick buildings that lined the street. Freshly planted flowers accompanied each building, highlighting various shades of red, yellow, and orange. Their aroma filtered through the morning air. Every shop had handcrafted columns and chiseled designs in brick and marble.

Wooden signs advertised the town's offerings: a hair salon, consignment shop, bakery, and bookstore. The town was quaint and charming. It unfolded like a picture book. Riley wished she and April could dive into one of its pages and live happily in the fantasy world. Though Riley could imagine how inviting the shops were during the day, the storefronts were completely dark, ruining her vision.

A car slowly rolled down the street, blocking Riley's view of the buildings. She followed the car's taillights and noticed a large clock towering over the buildings down the road. She squinted her eyes to focus on the hands of the old-timey analog clock.

"Six-ooooooh-seven, April," Riley exclaimed, looking down at the little girl who had been following a ladybug's trail across the bench. "Bug!" She shouted with excitement. Riley smiled as she picked up the ladybug and let it crawl around her finger. "Ooo!" April cheered. The ladybug unveiled its wings and flew down the street toward the clock tower.

"Bye-bye." April waved frantically.

"Let's follow it!" Riley encouraged, looking for a way to get April excited about walking for a bit.

"Yeah!" April agreed, shimmying off the bench. She reached above her head to grab Riley's hand as they made their way down the sidewalk.

With each step, more sunlight peered through the clouds and illuminated their feet.

They walked in silence through the town. April was focused on her own footsteps while Riley was focused on coming up with a plan. She was distracted by the essence of this fictitious-looking town and the rumbling of her stomach. As they approached the next block, a glimmer of light highlighted the cobblestone and reflected in the windows of the nearby shops.

"There's no way something is actually open, right, April?" April didn't respond, still fixating on her shoes. They walked a bit further, enough to turn the corner down Maiden Lane. Riley was attracted to the light like a moth to a bug zapper. She could feel her tugging on April's arm for her to speed up. She swept April up off her feet to move even quicker. As they approached the lit building, the sign above read: *The Cozy Cup - 24 Hour Diner*.

Riley's Cheshire smile turned sour when she remembered she had no money with her. She stood at the door with April for a moment, focusing her gaze on their reflection in the glass door.

"Eh. I'll figure it out." Riley opened the door cautiously. A small bell chimed as they stepped through. The diner was completely empty - a ghost town. No patrons or workers, just a bakery case filled to the brim with delicious cinnamon rolls, donuts, croissants, and macarons. The barstools were collecting dust, and the placemats looked like they had fused into the wooden tables.

"What kind of town are we in, April?" Riley questioned. April looked around, enamored by the funky lights hanging above the coffee bar.

"Hewwo?" April called throughout the diner. They waited for a response, but no answer. Riley stepped further into the establishment to explore. Light coffeehouse radio played through the ceiling, adding to the charming yet eerie ambiance. The smell of freshly brewed mocha filled the air, and Riley swooned at the thought of her first sip of a hot drink after a chilling, wet night. She walked to the back of the diner and peeked out the window to see if one of the workers was maybe taking a smoke break.

"Jeez, April. I won't last too long here. Everything smells so..." A hand calmly rested on Riley's shoulder. She flinched, throwing her body against the window, and shrieked.

"Oh! I didn't mean to startle you," said the woman, dressed in a blue button-up shirt and a brown apron with an embroidered coffee cup on the front. Riley stood silent, hopelessly trying to catch her breath. April clung to her shirt. The woman spoke again.

"I'm...I'm sorry I didn't greet you when you arrived. I was in the back, grabbing some fresh coffee beans. Welcome to the Cozy Cup! I'm Molly. You can sit anywhere you'd like." She flashed a kind smile as she walked behind the counter to grab the girls a menu.

After regaining her strength, Riley sat in the nearest booth, putting April in first. Molly rushed over and brought a few crayons for April to keep her occupied.

"Wow, thank you!" Riley grinned.

"Can I get you anything to drink? A coffee, maybe?" Molly asked, with her pen and paper in hand.

"I would really just love a water, please." She was unbelievably parched, like she'd just endured a week in the Sahara. "She'll take one too." She motioned to April.

"Of course!" Molly said, mindlessly tapping her pen on her notepad before disappearing behind the counter again. Riley looked down at the menu while April drew red and blue scribbles on a blank sheet of paper.

French toast with fresh whipped butter and powdered sugar; two eggs over medium with wheat toast and thick-cut bacon; a spinach, cheddar, and tomato omelet served with fresh fruit and shredded hash browns; fresh strawberry and banana smoothies; every coffee combination you could think of; and pastries made fresh every morning.

With no money to enjoy any of this delicious food, Riley felt like the universe was dangling a bright orange carrot in front of her face while she ran on a treadmill.

She looked down at April and stroked her curls. She was distracted now, but soon she'd be asking for a snack of some kind. Molly appeared tableside with the drinks. Riley's tall glass was filled to the brim with ice and garnished with an orange wedge. April's water came in a colorful glass with The Cozy Cup's logo and a bendy straw.

"Oh, April! How fun!" She slid the cup across the table in front of her. April immediately dropped her crayons to grip the glass. Riley watched as the water swirled and twirled through the loops of the straw and into April's mouth. Riley lunged for her cup and gulped down nearly half before motioning a 'thank you' to Molly.

"Wow! You both seem parched!" Molly exclaimed. "Do you need a few more minutes to look over the menu? I just took some fresh chocolate croissants out of the oven if you're interested!"

Riley looked around at all of the empty booths and tables. "Do you usually get a lot of people in the morning?"

"Mmm," Molly said, caught off guard. "Not usually for another hour or so. I work the night shift, so I'm usually by myself baking and filling the case for the next day. There are a few stragglers throughout the night, but not many! So…would you like a croissant?" She asked again.

"I'm…not sure yet. Can I have a few more minutes?" Riley graciously questioned.

"Absolutely! Just holler when you're ready."

Riley pretended to scan the menu items, but inside, she was panicking, wondering what the hell she was going to do to get a quick meal. Riley wasn't the dine-and-dash type, and Molly seemed incredibly genuine, but hunger consumed every inch of her thoughts.

"*What if I'm just honest with her?*" Riley questioned in her head. "*Oh, yeah, just tell her that you're running from your boss, who has gone absolutely insane after knocking you unconscious and tying you up, just so you can protect their kid, who,* news flash, *isn't even THEIRS. And even though you HAVE money, you don't have it with you right now and there's no way to get it, but you would just really love a stack of hot cakes.*" Riley hit her head with the flimsy laminated menu. "*Stupid Riley, you've gone completely stupid.*"

"Okay?" April asked Riley, having watched her outburst. Riley rubbed her back.

"Yes, yes. I'm okay. We're just gonna have to wing it…"

"Hey Molly?" Riley called to the back of the diner. She watched Molly plow through the double doors of the kitchen.

"I'll be there in one second, just finishing setting up the cold brew!" Molly said across the counter.

"Give her enough information to get what we want, but not enough to put us in any danger," Riley repeated in her head as she watched Molly pour coarse coffee grounds into a large glass pitcher, followed by a jug of filtered water.

After putting her mixture into a small fridge, she wiped her hands on her apron and approached their table once again.

"Alright! What can I get'cha?" She inquired politely, pen in hand.

"So, I'm in a bit of a predicament...would you mind sitting down with us for a moment?" Riley asked nervously.

"Uhh, sure!" Molly retorted, sitting across from them in the brightly colored booth. "I know there are lots of great things on the menu. I can give you some recommendations if you want!"

"Well, you see, little April and I have been homeless for the past few days. I ended up getting into a big fight with my..." Riley paused for a moment. "My mom. And she hasn't let us back in the house. We haven't eaten since yesterday morning, and we're running out of fresh water." She forced crocodile tears to well in her eyes.

"I have money; I swear to you, it's just at my mom's house. If you're willing to give us an I.O.U., I promise as soon as my mom lets me back in, I will pay triple the cost, with an extra tip!" Riley said, nearly begging. She held April close to her. "Even if you can't give anything to me, please find it in your heart to give something to my little April here."

Molly put down her pad of paper on the table. "I'm sorry she just…kicked you out like that. That's awful, especially when you have a baby. How heartless!" Her voice echoed with rage. Riley's theatrics were working.

"Yeah, she's a bit…you know." Riley motioned, swirling her finger around her temple.

"Wow, is…there anyone else that could help you? Family, friends?" Molly asked.

"Well, we're really not from around here, so at the moment, no." Riley hung her head in shame, flicking the sides of the laminated menu.

"Um, well, okay…You seem trustworthy. I'm not sure my boss is going to like this very much…but as long as you promise to come back and pay once your, uh, family matters are resolved, I'm happy to spot you a plate today." She flashed a side smile. Riley nearly sprang from her seat to smother Molly with hugs and kisses.

"You have no idea how much this means to me. You can trust me. Thank you, thank you, THANK YOU!" Riley emphasized. Molly stood up from the booth and took a deep breath.

172

"Okay, you two! I'll whip something up to fill both of your bellies. I'll be back in a jiffy!" And off she went, back through the double doors and into the kitchen. Riley turned to April and let out the biggest sigh of relief. April was still passionately drawing circles all over her sheet of paper.

"You ready to eat-eat, April?" Riley asked. She looked up from her paper with a smile that spread from ear to ear. She grabbed her cup once again and gulped down a big sip of water through her bendy straw.

Riley plucked the juicy orange wedge from the side of her cup and sank her teeth into the pulp. The acidity tingled her taste buds as she chewed on the segments. Riley pulled a small piece off for April. She slowly grabbed the orange with her thumb and index finger and studied it before popping it into her mouth. "There's more where that came from in just a few, April." The orange juice ran down her chin and onto her shirt.

"Hmmm, let's see if I have a bib in here for you, messy girl." Riley grabbed the diaper bag from the floor and plopped it on top of the table. She unzipped the largest compartment and rummaged through the contents. "I know there's one in here." She dug around blindly. She eventually resorted to taking everything out and displaying it on the table like she was at a yard sale.

Spare clothes went in one pile, and diapers in another. The two stuffed animals were quickly snatched up by April and given a loving embrace. Miscellaneous wrappers and empty bottles were thrown in one of the empty pockets.

Finally, toward the very bottom of the bag was April's bib. It was a terry-cloth texture, patterned with roses and daisies. It was stained from a previous meal. "This will do!" Riley said, pulling it out of the bag carelessly. Something flew out of the bag and smacked on the floor.

"Whoops!" Riley said, buttoning the bib around April's neck before leaning over the booth. She bent down and scanned the floor to look for what may have dropped, but couldn't find anything except a dusty straw wrapper and used chewing gum stuck underneath the table.

"*Hmm, maybe I just imagined dropping something?*" Riley thought to herself, shifting her weight back up on the booth.

She found a small popping toy in the diaper bag that she knew April would love. "Look what I found!" She declared, waving it in front of April's face. April squealed as she held out both hands to grab it. Another distraction was a win for Riley.

As she waited for her long-overdue meal, she looked past April and out the window, showcasing the small town. The sun was rising quickly, shining golden rays on the awnings and shutters of the buildings. Headlights filled the streets as people made their way to work on their morning commutes.

Closed signs began switching to open. Lights gleamed through the windows. Riley's mouth watered as the tantalizing smells of maple syrup and apple-smoked sausage filled the air. She turned back toward the coffee counter and saw Molly heading toward them with two large plates.

"Oh boy, April, get ready!" She whispered, nudging her playfully.

"Okay, ladies! We have some scrambled eggs, fruit, and mini French toast squares for the little one." Molly slid the plate in front of April. Her eyes grew to the size of the orange slice that was once on Riley's glass.

"And, for you, ma'am, we have the largest stack of hotcakes we serve, smothered in syrup, with sausage and fruit." Riley bent down to waft the warm smells further into her nose. Notes of sweet and savory danced through her senses. Her mouth salivated like a rabid dog.

She turned to hand April a fork so she could start digging into her eggs. Though she was still learning, Riley couldn't care less about April making a mess as long as she ate.

"Is there anything else I can get for you?" Molly asked.

Riley slowly looked the waitress in the eyes.

"No, Molly. This is more than enough, thank you." She picked up her fork and cut a huge chunk of pancake from the middle. The slab of melted butter fell through the crevice and onto the warm plate.

"No problem, just holler if you need me!" She turned to walk back toward the kitchen but stopped short. Riley hardly noticed as she was about to shove a buttery, syrupy stack of pancakes into her gullet. April was distracted by the pillowy soft eggs on her fork.

Molly bent down, picking something up off the floor, and turned around slowly toward the girls.

"A...mari Syke?" Molly queried, holding an orange pill bottle in her hand. Riley's body instantly shuddered at the sound of that name. Her vision went blurry, then crossed. Her fork stopped just short of her lips before it slipped out of her hand and onto the stack of pancakes. Her head slowly turned toward Molly's direction, her gaze crawling up her body before reaching her eyeline.

"Is that your name? Am I saying that right? Amari Syke?" She asked again, now holding the orange pill bottle out to Riley. Without losing eye contact, she slowly reached for the bottle while nodding her head.

"Th-thank...thank..." Riley focused. "Thank you. I...knew I had dropped something." Molly raised an eyebrow as she handed Riley the bottle before shrugging her shoulders and going back through the double doors into the kitchen.

The steam from the hotcakes smacked Riley's face as she held the tattered pill bottle with both hands. The same one she had found last night with the worn label. She slowly peeled back the corner of the label to reveal, in broad daylight, Amari Syke of 370 Sprulette Road.

Intense ringing blared in Riley's ears. The sounds of April chewing her breakfast were muffled, and she lost feeling in her fingers. Her stomach contracted with a wave of heat, followed by ice. Her thoughts became scrambled, just like April's eggs. She was a statue of pure confusion.

As Riley reread the faded letters over and over, she wondered how in the world Amari's medication bottle would have ended up in April's diaper bag. Riley studied April's features like never before. Her green eyes, her caramel skin, her dimpled ears. She leaned in closer toward her head, and noticed the roots of her hair, once an intense jet-black color, were growing in blonde.

At that moment, the fog surrounding the folds of Riley's brain started to dissipate. The sounds of coffee brewing replaced the ringing in her ears. Her vision sharpened as a wave of clarity washed over her body.

"How could I have been so naive?" Riley shouted to herself. April turned toward her with a mouth full of fruit. "Quincy nearly spelled it out to me," she spoke directly to April.

"The backyard, dyeing your hair, taking you to your dad's house instead of back to your mom because…she…was in jail. The woman at the pharmacy was…Amari. Your real mom." Realization set in, fast and hard. "YOUR REAL MOM IS AMARI. LAUREN. YOUR NAME IS LAUREN. YOU'RE LAUREN!" Riley yelped, hugging the girl tighter than she ever had before.

"Is…everything okay out here?" Molly wondered, poking her head through the double doors. Riley let out a nervous laugh.

"Ha, yes! So sorry, Laur…sorry. April and I just play a silly little game. Sometimes it gets a bit rowdy. We'll quiet down!" Molly nodded and went back to prepping for the day.

Riley stared back at the pill bottle in disbelief. "How could I have missed this?" She shook her head. Shame pricked her skin.

All this time, the clues hidden in plain sight were casually overlooked.

Misinterpretation was masked as the truth, and it took Riley this long, too long, to put the pieces together. In the midst of experiencing every emotion simultaneously, a sliver of ascertainment flooded her veins. She turned to April…Lauren…the little girl, who was still filling her belly, unaware of the scary, twisted world that she had been a part of. She bent down to whisper in her ear. "I'm going to bring you home to your mommy," she assured her with tears in her eyes.

April smiled at the sound of the word. "Mama!" She exclaimed as she bit into a piece of juicy, ripe honeydew. Dribbles soaked into her bib as she carelessly went in for another bite. Riley turned back toward her plate. *"How the hell am I going to do that? I have no idea,"* she thought. Riley shut down her thoughts for a few moments, long enough to get in a few bites of food. Her hunger had vanished entirely, but she knew she needed energy to get April back to a safe place, wherever that was.

——

After forcing down the entire plate of pancakes, three out of four sausage links, and all of her fruit except for the cherries, Riley's brain decided to clock back in.

April had stuffed her face as much as her little belly would allow and had returned to coloring shapes and scribbles on her paper.

Riley ran her hands through her hair, hoping to massage a clear thought from her head into existence.

"Do I take her straight to Rita while I figure out where Kendra went? Or do I call Amari first and ask her what she wants me to do? After all, it is her kid! No, no," Riley fought with herself, *"I need to make sure she's safe before I tell her. Amari's not going to know what to do."* Riley placed her face in her hands. *"Maybe I should just take her to the pol-"*

The bell on the door chimed, interrupting Riley's thoughts. She slowly removed her hands from her face as two suited officers walked into The Cozy Cup. Her eyes followed them as her body remained frozen. They looked around, just as Riley did when she first arrived with April. They started wandering toward the back of the cafe, and Riley slipped back into normalcy. She turned toward April, trying her best to conceal her face. After all, Riley's face had been plastered all over the news just a few weeks ago, claiming to aid in the disappearance of this very child. She didn't want the police to get any funny ideas.

Without looking at their table, the officers pulled two barstools and sat directly in front of their booth, only they were facing the coffee bar instead of Riley. One officer was older with a darker complexion, and his beard was peppered with gray hairs.

The other looked straight out of boot camp. His dark brown hair was gelled to the side, and his uniform looked freshly pressed. Molly promptly walked out to greet them. Riley moved her hair behind her ear to listen more closely.

"Hello, officers; what can I get for you today?" she said formally, less cordial than she was with Riley.

"Just two black hot coffees to go, " the older officer bellowed in a deep voice.

"Of course, coming right up." Molly disappeared under the bar to grab the to-go cups before filling them with freshly brewed coffee. "Coffee is on the house today. I appreciate everything that you do." Molly said robotically, fading back into the kitchen once again. Riley found the interaction odd. But she disregarded it to focus back on April and the situation at hand.

"*Now would be a perfect chance to ask for help.*" Riley's thoughts ping-ponged in her brain, unsure of the best approach. "*What would I even say? How do you even begin to position this? They're not even going to...*" Riley felt a warm tap on her left shoulder.

She smiled at April, who was looking past Riley and up at something. Riley turned around to see both officers towering over her.

Their gun belts, equipped with every weapon imaginable, were at her eye level. She swallowed the lump in her throat and looked up to greet them.

"Good morning officer..." she quickly read the name badge on his chest, "Nico. How are you both today?" Riley tried to make friendly conversation.

"That's Lieutenant, ma'am. We're doing well. We couldn't help but admire this pretty little girl with you! What's your name, sweetie?" He directed toward April.

"Well, that's complicated," Riley thought to herself before quickly answering. "April. This is April. Say hi, April!" Riley's palms oozed. The girl cowered behind Riley's arm, refusing to acknowledge them. "Sorry, she's a bit shy sometimes."

"No problem," they said.

An awkward silence fell over the table as the officers kept a watchful eye on April. Riley wasn't quite sure what else to say to them.

"Well, I, uh…Hope you both have a nice day. It looks like it's going to be beautiful out." Her cheeks flushed with color. She hoped they would get the hint to let them finish their breakfast.

"Yeah, yeah, it does! Hey, what did you say your name was again? I must have missed it." The officer asked Riley.

Without thinking, she blurted, "Oh! I don't believe you asked. My name is Ri…ley…"

Her voice morphed into slow motion, and the background blurred around the officers. As soon as she said her name, their eyes widened, and they placed their hands on their gun belts. Riley sank back into the booth, trying to act coy.

"Is… there something wrong?" Riley asked.

"Ma'am, is there a chance you and April could step outside with us, just for a moment? We have a few questions we'd like to…ask you." They stepped back from the table.

"Oh, uh, sure, of course. Whatever you need!" Riley awkwardly slid out of the booth. April clung to her arm like a monkey on a tree branch.

She hoisted April up onto her hip and collected all of her crayons and toys. The officers began to walk toward the front door, and Riley followed.

"CUP!" April yelped. Riley quickly turned around to grab April's sippy cup. As she walked through the cafe, she looked through the small portholes on the double doors and saw Molly peeking through. She cracked the door open slightly. "Have a nice day, officers," Molly called to them, slinking back behind the doors.

"Appreciate you, Molly. We'll be in touch," they hollered back as they opened the front door.

"*Appreciate her for what?*" Riley pondered, whipping her head back toward the kitchen. Molly had disappeared.

"*There's no way she would have called the cops on me. Why would she have done that? She agreed to let me come back and pay...I don't get it.*"

Riley and April marched through the door and out onto the sidewalk. Two police cars were parked on the curb. Riley noted a bright, reflective sticker on the back of the car that said K-9. She gulped and gripped April closer to her body.

Lieutenant Nico opened the passenger-side door of one of the cars and grabbed a large notepad and a pen. The younger officer refused to look at Riley. His eyes were locked on April. Riley's body tensed. She was desperate to break the ice.

"Sir, I'm happy to help with whatever you need, but could you tell me what's going on?" She asked cowardly. The men remained silent. Lieutenant Nico was frantically writing notes on his pad.

"This…this isn't about me not paying for breakfast, right? The waitress, Molly, and I spoke and agreed it was fine for me to come back later. I'm sure if you just go in and talk with her, this is all just one big misunder-"

"Ma'am, please calm down," Lieutenant Nico said, as he looked up from his pad. A shiver slid down Riley's back. She sucked her lips back towards her teeth to prevent any more words from escaping. "Now listen, you're not in trouble or anything. We just want to talk."

"Yes, sir. What would you like to talk about?"

He looked down at April, then back at Riley.

"Molly seemed a bit concerned about you and your…daughter?"

"No, no, she's not my daughter. I'm just her nanny."

"Got it." He dismissed. "Well, based on your demeanor, Molly was a bit frightened for your safety. She noted your clothes were covered in dirt, you didn't have any money to pay for breakfast, and you just seemed skittish when speaking with her. She said you looked familiar, like she had seen you on TV or something."

"*Gee, and I thought Molly was cool*," Riley thought to herself before refocusing on the lieutenant.

"Coincidentally, we received a call from an extremely concerned mother this morning about a missing child. One with dark curly hair, light skin, and goes by the name of..."

"April." The younger officer joined in, finally making eye contact with Riley.

Riley's heart sank through her body and down into the earth below her feet. Her legs trembled at the thought of another setup. The theories that ran through the officers' minds at that moment couldn't be further from the truth. Riley slowly stepped closer toward them and lowered April's head onto her chest, lightly covering her ear to muffle her hearing.

"You may know of me, and you more than likely don't trust me. But I'm begging you to listen. My name is Riley Michaels. Yes, the same Riley Michaels you've probably seen all over the news and talked for hours about in your squad meetings.

I have been framed on more than one occasion for putting this little girl in danger, but all of the theories are wrong. I will tell you absolutely everything I know about this situation. No detail left untold, on one condition. You cannot give this child back to the woman who called in this morning. You would be putting April's life in immense danger. You don't understand what we've been through in the past few days...hell, the past few weeks, months! Give me fifteen minutes, that's all I ask, and I will explain everything." Riley's body was still tense with fear. She rubbed her hand against April's back to prevent herself from having a panic attack. The officers must have seen the twinkle of desperation in her eyes. Or maybe they were simply curious about the story she was going to tell.

"You've got 15 minutes, Ms. Michaels." Lieutenant Nico ordered, opening the back door of the police car. He motioned for Riley and April to get in. Riley followed his orders. After sitting down, he promptly slammed the door, startling April.

"It's okay, sweets," Riley assured. "Just hang in there a little longer."

The back of the cop car was dark and musty. Tattered rips in the leather seats clearly indicated previous struggles. Splatters of dried spit coated the semi-frosted plexiglass separating the front from the back. The officers opened the front doors and flopped into their seats. The car was silent for a few moments before Riley worked up the courage to speak.

"Let me start from the beginning…"

———

Over the next fifteen minutes, Riley felt like a machine. Hardly taking a breath, she told the officers everything that had happened, including every gruesome detail. Kendra's horrible crime and Quincy's willingness to be an accomplice. The lies, the deceit, the murders. She begged them to go back to April's father's house to recover his and Quincy's bodies and to prove the legitimacy of her story. She told them about Amari, the random Healix receipt at the swing set, the pill bottle, and April's true identity.

Regardless of what happened to Riley, she begged them to take April back to Rita. She knew she would be the only person other than herself to keep April safe. Through her words, Riley felt flustered and desperate for them to trust her and, even more so, for them to keep April away from Kendra.

The car fell silent once again. The men looked at each other without saying a word. They both opened their doors simultaneously and stepped out. She leaned forward from her seat. Looking through the rearview mirror and the tinted glass, Riley could vaguely see them talking and speaking into their walkie-talkies. The soundproof doors muffled their voices to the point where they sounded like they were speaking underwater.

"Did they believe me?" Riley wondered. *"Are they calling in back-up to go to April's dad's house? Or, back-up to take...me back to jail?"*

She could feel her pancakes sliding back up her throat. Acid burned the back of her tongue. She swallowed the bile and tried her best to focus on her breathing. Cuddling with April helped. Still oblivious, she began playing with Riley's matted, orange hair. She lifted one side, then the other, to make it look like a wave rippling on the shore. Riley smiled as April giggled. Just then, the front door swung open. Lieutenant Nico sat down in the driver's seat, while the younger officer remained outside.

"Here's what we're going to do, Ms. Michaels. We're going to go to this house you spoke of. The one where Kendra supposedly shot two people."

"We?" Riley questioned.

"We," the lieutenant replied bluntly. "You're coming with me."

"What about April? I'm not leaving her again."

"She is going to stay with my partner, Officer Cooper until we finish the investigation. He's going to take her down to the station."

"Sir, I am not trying to be confrontational, but I need you to give me your word that she will not be given back to Kendra. That you won't even contact her until I prove to you that my story is true."

Riley was more confident than before. The officer looked back through the plexiglass and into her eyes.

"Kendra will not know that we have her in custody. You have my word."

Riley nodded, and Lieutenant Nico motioned his partner to open the back door. Riley hopped out with April. She looked at Officer Cooper, who had his arms out to take the little girl. His demeanor had completely switched.

"Listen, it sounds like you've been through a lot over the past few weeks. This can't be easy for you. But she will be in the best hands, I promise. I have three nieces who are like daughters to me. We will not let anything happen to her." He said empathetically.

"Can I have a moment to talk with her, please?" Riley said with tears in her eyes.

"Sure, of course." He walked back toward the front of the car to talk to Lieutenant Nico.

Riley sat down on the ground and faced April. She looked confused as she watched tears pour from Riley's eyes. April reached up to touch the teardrops and rubbed the drips around her fingertips. Riley searched for the right words to say if there even were any. With her being nearly two, nothing about this situation was going to make sense.

"April, I need you to know that I love you."

"Wuv yew," April leaned in to give Riley a kiss. Their lips touched, and Riley sprang to cradle her little body in her arms.

"You're going to go play with the nice police officers for a bit. And I will be back really, really soon, okay?" She whispered in her ear.

"Bye-bye?" April questioned.

"Yeah, kiddo," Riley trembled. "But not for long, okay? And soon, we'll play again, eat ice cream, watch your favorite shows, and snuggle, okay?"

April laid her head on Riley's chest, seemingly understanding her words. Riley lifted them both up and approached the officer again.

"No Kendra." Riley repeated.

"No Kendra." Officer Cooper confirmed.

Riley reluctantly handed April and her diaper bag over. She squirmed in his arms, wincing and moaning to get down and back to Riley. The noises sparked flashbacks of putting April in Quincy's car just weeks ago. She closed her eyes tightly in hopes of resetting her mind.

"I'll be back soon, April, I promise," she said, walking back toward Lieutenant Nico's car. She touched the handle of the door and looked back at April, who was beginning to calm down.

Officer Cooper pulled one of her stuffed animals from her bag and was doing everything he could to make her smile. This set Riley at ease, enough to get in the car at least. She stepped in and clicked her seatbelt into place. The officer did the same and placed both hands on the steering wheel.

"Do you know where we're going?" Lieutenant Nico asked. Riley thought for a moment. She did everything she could to recount her drive with Quincy. The overwhelming number of trees, the people watching from their porches, and the no outlet sign. "*Think, Riley, think!*"

"Shady Show? Shallow...? South...SHORE. South Shore Trailer Park. I will guide you from there." Riley was stunned by her own memory.

"That's not far from here, just a few miles away." He grabbed his walkie-talkie and clicked the button on the side. "Signal seven and have 'em step up." He put the car in drive and sped away from the diner.

"*That sounds serious.*" She twisted her head around to look out the rear window as Lieutenant Nico pulled away.

Riley watched as April, the girl she had risked her entire life for, faded into the distance once again.

whodunit

The stale air triggered memories of Riley in the back of the police car last month. Though she was hardly coherent then, she remembered the feeling of the sticky leather seats against her legs and the "shatterproof glass" sticker that sat catty-cornered on the edge of the window. But this time was different. Fear slowly faded into focus. She fought through the web of lies and successfully untangled them, thread by thread.

Riley picked and peeled the skin from her thumb, something she often did when unsettled. Subtly shaking her head, she sat on her hands to prevent further self-destruction. Clouded glass separated Lieutenant Nico and Riley, making her feel like a lonely animal trapped in a zoo enclosure.

She tracked beads of sweat on his forehead and his twitching fingers against the steering wheel. His eyes never deviated from the road in front of him. Suddenly, his words bounced through the metal grates on the sides of the glass and into Riley's ears.

"So...Riley, can we talk off the record?" Lieutenant Nico said over his shoulder.

She chuckled to herself after hearing that phrase. She felt like she had been transported into a stereotypical cop-drama TV show.

She didn't know much about the justice system, but she knew that she'd already waived her Miranda Rights by telling them everything about Quincy and Kendra, so what did she have to lose?

"Sure, Lieutenant."

"So, with everything you've been through, you seem pretty composed. You know, witnessing one murder and being convinced of the other seems quite intense. After you escaped into the woods with April last night, why didn't you call for help, seek out the police...anything?" His tone felt sharp and targeted.

The car fell silent. Riley wasn't quite sure how to respond. Explanations swirled in her brain like a tornado.

"Sir, the last few months have been full of firsts for me. I moved to Clarendon Hills after my mom tragically died. I became a nanny only because I needed something to fill the void from my nearly failed writing career. Just when I thought things were finally looking up for me, I was framed for a horrible crime against the person I loved most in the world and thrown into an environment where I was forced to survive completely on my own. Add in the constant thoughts of April's whereabouts, with the bombshell of Quincy and Kendra's scheme, and solving an ongoing missing person case, all in the span of a few months?" Riley gasped for air, pausing to catch her breath and reel in her theatrics.

"I think after the gunshots and running for my life all night long, I just needed a break. I was craving normalcy and…pancakes, quite honestly. I knew the right thing to do was to go to the police, and frankly, that's what I had planned to do right after we left the diner. But with little knowledge about the town, no transportation, and truly nobody to trust…" Riley stopped again and was now staring at the floor. "I was scared. Scared that nobody would believe me. That…that I would end up back in jail to rot away while Kendra and Quincy continue to ruin this little girl's life, and everyone tangled in it."

Her hands caressed her tears as she composed her thoughts. She looked back up through the glass and into the Lieutenant's eyes in the rear-view mirror.

"Some days, you feel like the ocean. Other days, you feel like it's swallowing you whole. Last night I was searching for my water wings, but this morning, you and your partner unknowingly showed up with a life vest." Lieutenant Nico didn't say a word. Left turn, after right turn. Stop light after stop sign. Silence. She stared out the window until the view became familiar.

"There! That's the trailer park. Turn here." Riley shouted. Lieutenant Nico turned sharply, hopping the curb and just barely clearing the welcome sign. The trailer park looked even worse in the daylight.

A thick coating of algae and moss covered the siding of all the trailers, and jagged rust looked like a second coat of paint on the awnings. Tangled clothing lines with mismatched socks and underwear hung out in the sun to dry. Sun-bleached front doors were plastered with "*NO SOLICITING*" signs. A brown-and-black spotted dog stood in the front yard next to Travis's trailer. The pup's ribs were noticeable, even from a distance and under his matted fur.

Lieutenant Nico pulled his car onto the grass in front of the trailer, completely bypassing the empty driveway. Riley noticed three small oil splotches on the pavement where Kendra's car was parked the night before.

Shortly after the car was put in park, an unmarked police car pulled up in front of theirs. Even in the daylight, the flashing blue-and-red lights from Lieutenant Nico's hood reflected off the surrounding trailers.

Riley watched as three officers hustled out of the unmarked vehicle, guns drawn. Her heart pounded against her fragile chest. She slowly looked toward Lieutenant Nico, who was now staring back at her.

"Ms. Michaels, you're gonna stay close to me. Got it?"

"Understood."

Riley sat patiently, waiting for him to open her door. She gripped her toes in her still-damp shoes and took a calming breath. The door clicked open, and Riley slid out onto the grass.

The other officers looked at her with confusion, but quickly disregarded her and continued sneaking around the outside of the trailer. She followed closely behind the Lieutenant, who walked right up to the front door.

"It's locked," Riley called while he jiggled the handle. The Lieutenant scoffed and walked back down the concrete steps, nearly slipping on the cracked pavement. He walked past her and toward the back of the trailer, motioning for her to follow. As they rounded the side, she noticed her makeshift stool was still by the open window.

The Lieutenant looked at the window and then down at the bricks. He almost spoke to Riley, but before he could say a word, the radio on his hip exploded with orders and codes from other officers.

"0110, 0142. 1 Burnham Street. 0110, 0142. 1 Burnham Street." Lieutenant Nico broke into a full sprint. Riley tried her best to keep up. The officers crowded the back door, stunned at their findings. Lieutenant Nico pushed through the officers to see what they were gawking at.

To his surprise, there was Travis, just as Riley saw him the night before. The blood from his open wound had crusted to the floor and around his hair. It seeped deeply into the crevices of the wooden floorboards. The stench of his freshly decaying body rampaged through the home and out the door.

Lieutenant Nico repeated the same codes into his radio with even more panic and urgency. The remaining three officers poured into the house like the flood gates had burst, guns steady in front of their bodies. They kicked in the doors and screamed through the home to see if anyone was hiding.

Judging by the stains in the driveway, Kendra was long gone. Riley chose to stay outside, knowing she couldn't stomach seeing Travis's body up close again. She crossed her arms and stared at her shoes, listening to the officer's panic as they ransacked the home. Suddenly, a pair of boots came into her view, and her head lifted quickly.

"Riley, you said there were two."

"I'm sorry?"

"You said two people were murdered last night."

Oh. Quincy. How could she have forgotten? Her eyes widened as she realized she had never actually seen him get shot.

"As I told you, sir, I heard Quincy yell through the tree line, and then two shots were fired. I assumed Kendra shot him point-blank because they were both outside of the trailer. But I can't be certain that she actually hit him. I just never heard his voice after that," Riley said, rubbing her wrists.

"Hmpf." Lieutenant Nico said, looking around. He swiftly turned and ran back into the home without saying another word. Not that Riley was looking for the Medal of Honor, but she would have loved a tiny bit of affirmation for bringing them to the scene of a very obvious homicide.

That conversation did make her wonder - *where the hell was Quincy*? Though it would have made perfect sense for Kendra to have shot him that night, Riley had no evidence to prove it. While the officers were busy with Travis and waiting for backup, Riley patrolled the backyard. She simulated the path she ran the night before and tried to predict where Kendra and Quincy would have ended up outside the home. Riley was discovering new information about Kendra's character each day, but she knew she was decently smart and probably tracked her into the trees.

"*She would have followed after me,*" Riley thought quietly, analyzing the ground with each step. She was clearly free from Quincy's clutches when she made her way outside. He more than likely struggled to gain control back.

"But how close would that have been to the trees?" She wondered.

Wandering with purpose, her steps led her closer and closer to where she entered the forest until she felt something sticky on her shoe. Looking down at her foot, she scraped whatever it was onto the grass. She lifted her foot to look at the bottom. It was covered in a gooey, brownish substance. Her head whipped around to look at where she'd walked. There was a noticeable dark brown splotch that saturated the grass.

Riley's heart palpitated. Her hands shook, and fear shivered down her spine, knowing that Quincy's blood was covering the bottom of her shoe. "Lieutenant Nico," she hollered across the backyard, unable to move another muscle. None of the officers heard her shriek. Panicking more at the thought of another death, she shouted louder. "Lieutenant NICO!"

Two officers came flying out the back door. They looked around to see where the shouting was coming from. Riley waved the officers down, and they swiftly came to her side. "Is everything alright, ma'am?" one of the officers asked, confused by her outburst. Riley was too stunned to speak. She pointed down at the patch of grass, and immediately, both officers stumbled back. One officer reached down to his radio.

"ETA on 0110 to 1 Burnham? Ev-evidence f-f-found." His voice trembled with each word. Hearing the words on the radio triggered Lieutenant Nico to rush outside to meet the other officers. Riley's eyes slammed shut as the sound of the bang she heard the night before replayed in her mind. Lieutenant Nico crouched down to the patch to observe it more closely. The smell must have been all he needed because he immediately stood back on his feet.

"MaCatty, go grab me an evidence bag. Stanton, head back to the house and await instructions."

MaCatty nodded and ran toward his car. Stanton recoiled. "Yes, sir, thank you," he said, cowardly. He was a younger-looking officer. Maybe this was his first homicide.

"I hate to do this to you, but I'm going to need your shoes." Lieutenant Nico pointed to her feet without hesitation.

"My shoes?" Riley questioned.

"Well, since there is blood on them, we need to…"

Riley shuttered. "You know what, I'm happy to give them over."

Officer MaCatty arrived with the bag, and Riley carefully slipped the damp shoes from her feet, exposing her dingy grey socks.

"Riley, can you come with me, please?"

"Of course," Riley said, following Lieutenant Nico closely. He repeated a slew of codes into his walkie-talkie.

She was thankful to distance herself from the patch of blood. He led her toward his police car. When they arrived, he opened the back door and motioned for her to get in. Slightly confused, Riley didn't bother questioning what he was doing. The radio blared with frantic police codes that she couldn't understand. The door opened, and Lieutenant Nico flopped down. He slowly turned toward Riley.

"I think we have more than enough evidence here to prove you were telling the truth."

It was definitely the wrong time, but Riley couldn't help but impulsively smirk at his remarks. "*FINALLY!*" She thought, trying her best to conceal her smile. "So, now what happens?"

"Would you like the by-the-book answer or what I'm envisioning?" Lieutenant Nico asked as he scratched the back of his head. Riley pondered for a moment, unsure of how different the two answers could be.

"I guess…what…you envision?" She hesitated.

"You obviously know more about this situation than any one of us. You're the key to solving this, Riley."

"That may be true…but that still doesn't fully answer my question, sir,"

"How far are you willing to go to ensure April's safety?"

Riley looked Lieutenant Nico dead in the eyes and, without hesitation, blurted out the first thought that came to her mind.

"I am willing to do whatever is necessary."

"I'm happy to hear you say that. I have a few ideas that I think would be best discussed down at the station with the rest of our detectives. We need to wait here until backup arrives. Then you and I will go down together. Sound good?" He asked.

Nothing about this situation sounded good to Riley, but if it meant April was safe, there wasn't much that Riley wouldn't do at this point.

"Yes. I'm in." Riley said confidently. "But, will you find me a new pair of shoes first?"

———

The ride to the police station was less tense than the trip to Travis's trailer, but just as uncomfortable. Even with Riley now being perceived as "one of the good guys", she was still hesitant about her newfound relationship with the officers.

Riley listened to Lieutenant Nico speak gibberish police codes the whole ride. She wondered what plans the officers had for her. Surely it was going to end with her and Kendra being in the same room again, and the thought of that reality made her stomach flip-flop like she was on a rollercoaster.

Lieutenant Nico turned down a side street and pulled up to the back of a brick building before putting the car in park. He promptly got out and opened Riley's door.

She scooted from her seat, and he guided her up to two metal doors. He flashed his badge against the black box attached to the wall, and the doors immediately opened to a sterile white hallway.

The walls were lined with professional portraits of captains, lieutenants, and officers from past years. They all had the same red, white, and blue backgrounds, and their hats were slightly cockeyed, triggering Riley's OCD.

Lieutenant Nico put his arm around Riley's shoulders as they marched down the hall. "I know your last experience with us wasn't pleasant. But I promise you, we're on the same team now."

Riley felt slightly uncomfortable and was unsure of what to say. "Uh, yeah. Happy to…be here?" Her cheeks flushed with color from her awkward comment. She looked down at her feet for the remainder of their walk. Her faded socks grazed the white tiled floor, which was scuffed with black smudges. This insignificant detail reminded her of the scratchy floor in Triple C.

Toward the end of the hallway, Lieutenant Nico walked Riley to a conference room. The windows were tinted, and the door was locked. With a quick flash of his badge, the door swung open, and there sat three men in large, black leather rolling chairs. One man was the same officer she had met at the diner earlier that day.

Papers, sticky notes, and folders were scattered across the glossy wooden table. Riley immediately noticed her driver's license photo next to Kendra's and Quincy's, with a picture of April underneath. As she walked in closer, she recognized April's clothes in the image. They were the same clothes she had on when she left her at the diner. Riley's eyes immediately met the officers. Sweat pooled as hot flashes surged through her body.

"Where is she?" Riley blurted out. The other officers were stunned to hear her speak so quickly.

"She's safe. I promised, remember?" Officer Cooper chuckled and swiveled his chair to look at the other men. His smile faded when he witnessed the fire in Riley's eyes.

"Where...is she?" Riley asked again, more directly this time, stepping closer to the table.

"Ms. Michaels, we have a unit that provides temporary housing for missing and exploited children. She's under their care and secured in this very building. There is nothing you need to be worried about." The other officers nodded in agreement, and the tension in Riley's shoulders melted.

"Gentleman, Ms. Michaels has agreed to help us with this investigation. Riley, this is Officer Wellington, Panella, and Cooper, who you met at the diner. Can you all catch her up to speed on what you've discussed so far?" Lieutenant Nico directed toward the men. "Please, Riley, have a seat."

Riley walked around the opposite end of the table and gently sat in the leather chair, which nearly swallowed her whole.

"We haven't gotten very far, Nico." Officer Panella said, moving a few papers on the table.

"Yeah, we have no idea of Kendra's whereabouts. We just sent officers to patrol her neighborhood, her husband's pharmacy, and Riley's residence." Officer Wellington said.

Even during a time like this, the sheer thought of officers surrounding Riley's home made her wonder if Griddle was scared half to death. He could hardly handle a thunderstorm, let alone 10 policemen marching up and down the driveway.

"Riley?" Lieutenant Nico called.

Her focus snapped back to attention. "Sorry, what was that?" Riley asked.

"Do you know of anywhere else that Kendra could be hiding? Does she have any family members or friends she may have run to?"

"No," Riley said sternly. "None of her family or friends know the truth. She would never drag her own name through the mud. She's running on her own, no doubt."

"But what about Quincy?" Officer Cooper asked, holding up his picture.

"That, I don't know. Kendra must have hidden his body somewhere." Riley stared into Kendra's eyes in her driver's license photo.

"Unless he wasn't the one who was shot." Officer Panella said slowly.

"What do you mean?" Riley pondered.

"Well, from what you told Nico, you didn't actually see the second shot, right?"

"Well, yeah, but Kendra…had the gun…?" Her sweaty fingers gripped the sides of her thighs as her chest tightened.

"When she was in the house, yes. But didn't Quincy restrain her? That's when you made your escape?" Officer Wellington chimed in. "It's not out of the realm of possibility."

Riley's eyebrows raised at the thought of Quincy still being alive and Kendra's blood being scattered over the lawn of Travis' trailer. She sank deeper into her chair and buried her chin in her chest.

"If that's the case, do we see Quincy as an immediate threat?" Lieutenant Nico asked.

"Yes!" All three officers chimed in.

"He…he saved my life," Riley spoke quietly, taken aback by her own words.

"Riley, he was an accomplice to a kidnapping, wrongly put you in jail, and potentially murdered his wife. He's completely unstable and a danger to society."

"You're right," Riley started. "But Kendra would have done anything to get April back from me, even if that meant putting a bullet in my skull. I wouldn't be sitting in this room if he weren't there that night. He drove me exactly to where she was. His guilt is overpowering, whatever demon possessed him to go along with this in the first place," she said, repositioning herself in her chair to look at the papers on the table.

"She may have a point, Nico." Officer Panella said reluctantly.

"Nothing is for certain yet. I think we should-"

The metal door burst open, interrupting Lieutenant Nico's thoughts. "Sorry to barge in like this, guys. But Lieutenant, I need you. The press is going absolutely insane over this story. News vans are parked at the trailer park entrance, and helicopters are flying overhead. We need to release a statement immediately," the frantic woman said, gripping a padfolio to her chest.

"Riley, I have to deal with this. Keep brainstorming, and I'll be back shortly," The Lieutenant said. He rushed out of the room and left Riley there with no allies.

"I...I think we need to come up with two different plans. One if Quincy is alive, and one if Kendra is alive." Riley shuddered. "Finding Kendra is our number one priority, right? I say we try to track her down first."

"Easier said than done, huh, Ms. Michaels?" Officer Wellington snickered. "How do you propose we do that?"

Riley thought for a moment. Her thoughts raced through her mind like cars on a track. Through the noise of the other officers talking amongst themselves, a moment of clarity shone through the clouds behind her eyes.

"I got it," Riley said, slamming her hands down on the table. She looked up at the officers, who were stunned by her sudden epiphany. "What's the one thing Kendra has been pining for this whole time?" Riley asked the men.

"April. Well, uh, Lauren. Uh…what are we calling her now?"

Riley shook her head in a frenzy of frustration. "April. She is desperate to get April back. Her mind is so consumed with the thought of having her perfect family that if we play our cards right, she'll slip up and get sloppy."

"Sloppy?" Officer Wellington asked.

"Think about it. She has no idea I'm working with you guys. And she knows I would never run to you first because, well, the justice system left a pretty sour taste in my mouth. You know, because of the whole wrongful imprisonment thing." Riley could feel herself start to ramble.

"Where are you going with this?" Officer Cooper asked bluntly.

"Things escalated rather quickly the last time I was at Kendra and Quincy's. But I do know that before I made a run for the door, I left my phone and purse on the dining room table. April and I will go back to the house, and if the phone is still where I left it, I'll call her. I'll beg her to come and take April from me because I'm not fit to take care of her or whatever stupid lie I have to tell to convince her."

Riley started pacing around the room. "Maybe I'll tell her I...I forgive her for everything she's done, and I just want us to go back to the way things were." Riley started to smile. She turned back toward the officers. "She'll fall for it and come back to the house...where your team will be waiting to cuff her." She crossed her arms, feeling proud of herself.

"You don't think...after murdering two people, that she doesn't know the police are already lurking around her home?" Officer Wellington said smugly.

Riley's flamboyance faded quickly. "Yeah, you're probably right."

"And why would April have to go with you? Wouldn't that put her in more danger?" Officer Panella asked genuinely.

"Kendra's smarter than you give her credit for. She'll want proof that I actually have April with me, and it's not a set-up."

"I don't think the concept is a bad idea." Officer Cooper chimed in. The other officers looked at him sideways. "She's not wrong about Kendra wanting the kid. If she's desperate enough, she'll take the bait. We just have to get her to trust us... Trust Riley." The men turned to look at Riley, who was now slumped in her leather chair.

"Now, what if Quincy is alive?" Officer Wellington piped up again.

After thinking for a moment, Riley came to an uncomfortable realization. "If you want my honest opinion, if he's still alive, he's probably long gone," Riley assured. "He willingly gave April back to Travis despite knowing how Kendra would react. If he were the one who shot Kendra, he'd have no incentive to stick around. If his name were tied to any of this, he'd lose everything he's ever worked for. And knowing him for just a short while, I don't think he would take that risk." The room fell silent. "I would have no idea where to even start looking for him. At least with Kendra, we know we have something she wants."

"Then we focus on finding her first and work backward," Officer Panella suggested. The room fell awkwardly silent, not knowing where to start.

"Do you know when Lieutenant Nico is coming back?" Riley wondered.

"It could be a while. The politics surrounding law enforcement are something we can't take lightly, especially in a situation like this." Officer Wellington said. Riley sank into her seat.

"Riley, would you like water or a snack? Anything?" Officer Cooper asked.

"No, I'm fine." She lied, fighting with her own thoughts. "On second thought, I would really love a glass of water. Thank you."

"Why don't you stretch your legs for a minute? Come grab it with me, I'll show you around. Maybe I can find you a pair of shoes, too." He motioned for her to follow him.

"Nico asked us to keep her here, Cooper." Officer Wellington forcefully called.

"Relax, man, she's been through some shit today. Let her breathe for a minute." He turned back to Riley. "It's ok, just follow me." Officer Cooper walked through the metal door.

She followed the officer through the threshold and briefly looked back at the officers, who quickly started reviewing the papers on the table again. "This way." Officer Cooper encouraged Riley to match his speed. She doubled her steps to catch up to him.

They walked down the sterile hallway until they reached a drab, dark, medium-sized lobby. The back wall was lined with chairs. A woman and a man sat uncomfortably next to each other and followed Riley with their eyes as she moved through the room. As she turned the corner to follow Officer Cooper, she saw a counter protected by a thick sheet of glass. It resembled a fishbowl. Through the tinted glass, she saw people working on computers. They briefly looked up to acknowledge Officer Cooper walking by.

"Cooper." One worker said uninterestedly before returning to his typing.

"Hello, Palmer." He retorted.

Riley avoided eye contact and kept close to Officer Cooper. He led her through another hallway and yet another set of doors until they reached a small room filled with uniforms. Riley stood in the doorway, still embarrassingly shoeless, as Office Cooper began rummaging through boxes.

"What's your size, Ms. Michaels?" He questioned.

"Seven, on a good day," Riley responded.

After a few more moments of digging, he pulled out a pair of shiny dress shoes.

"Am...am I allowed to wear those? They look too fancy." She asked timidly.

"Would you rather stay barefoot?" He chuckled.

"No…No, definitely not." She said, taking the shoes from Officer Cooper's hands and lacing them up. After settling into her new footwear, he led them both to the office kitchen.

Motivational posters of mountains and waterfalls are scattered on the walls. One poster read: *"The pain you feel today will be the strength you feel tomorrow."*

"Give me a break," Riley muttered under her breath. Officer Cooper swiftly walked to the fridge. A chilling voice startled him as he reached for the handle and stopped his movements.

"Riley?" The voice questioned. She slowly turned to acknowledge the speaker. Her heart sank at the sight of his face. In the back corner of the kitchen sat a man dressed in a freshly pressed navy suit with a light blue-and-orange tie. His brunette hair was perfectly combed and gelled to the side. A hint of his gold watch peeked from his sleeves. His expression was concerned, confused, and curious.

"I…what…what are you doing here? You're supposed to be in jail!" His voice vibrated with anger.

"I'm not sure how much you know, but…" Riley said, just before she was interrupted by the man.

"I know that you're the reason our sweet April is missing. How the hell did you get out?" Frustration echoed off the walls.

"Jared, I was bailed out, okay? I'm working very closely with these nice officers here," she said, pointing to Officer Cooper, "to find out where she is as fast as we can, okay? What are you doing here?" Riley asked nervously, stepping back closer to Officer Cooper.

"Training." He barked. "Is...is Kendra here? Does she know you're out? Is she working with you? Do you have any leads?" He demanded answers as he frantically adjusted the watch on his wrist.

"Look, I really can't talk about this. I'm sure you understand. I know how much this means to the family."

"Yeah, you've got that right. I talked to Kendra last night on the phone, and she sounded like an absolute train wreck." Riley's ears perked up like a dog.

"*She's alive. I knew it.*" She thought to herself. "Oh yeah?" Riley said, trying to play coy.

"Yeah, she's staying at the Hampton Inn down the street over the next few days. Said something about a bug problem at her house and needed to bomb it...I don't know. She sounded really stressed out about it."

"Oh yeah," Riley had to think quickly on her feet. "She mentioned that to me, too, a few months ago. Glad she's, uh, finally getting it taken care of." A bead of sweat formed on Riley's brow, and her hands were noticeably shaking.

Jared noticed her obscure body movements, and a scowl formed on his face again. "When will we know more information? This is my niece we're talking about. And Kendra hasn't kept me in the loop." He growled, adjusting in his chair.

"Sir," Officer Cooper chimed in. "I will ensure that the family is the first to know when we find something worth sharing. Until then, we really need to get back to this investigation." He quickly grabbed a bottle from the fridge and put his arm around Riley. They walked back through the kitchen and out the door.

"Was...was that Kendra's brother?" Officer Cooper whispered to Riley as they shuffled back to the conference room. Her chest was on the verge of collapse as she nodded in agreement. The two carried themselves back down the hallway. "Shit." Officer Cooper whispered. They walked in silence until they reached the other officers.

"Act natural." Officer Cooper said before opening the door. A large voice exploded as they walked through.

"Where have you two been?" Lieutenant Nico barked, standing up from his leather chair.

Riley turned white as a ghost at the thought of lying to an officer. "We went to grab a bottle of water; she was thirsty and needed a pair of shoes." Officer Cooper avoided Nico's eye contact as he sat back in his chair. Riley stood at the entrance of the room, frozen. She clicked the plastic of the water bottle lid as she begged her legs to move.

"Riley...?" The lieutenant questioned.

Silence settled in the room before Riley blurted about her encounter. "Kendra is alive, and I know where we can find her."

cigarette daydream and
the spare key

Riley and the officers huddled in the conference room for nearly an hour after she returned from her impromptu field trip to the break room. Initially, Lieutenant Nico was furious at Officer Cooper, but his temper cooled quickly when he heard about Jared and the potential of locating Kendra.

Questions of Jared's legitimacy circulated through the room as Officer Cooper frantically wrote the swirling details on a whiteboard in bright blue marker.

His shoes squeaked against the linoleum floor as he sharply spun around, an epiphany proudly brightening his expression.

"Wait a minute. I know a foolproof way to prove Jared's story. I have a buddy who works in security at the Hampton. While we wait for the official warrant, I can head that way to see what information I can squeeze out of them." He capped his marker and set it on the edge of the whiteboard.

Lieutenant Nico stared blankly, almost as if he was looking through him. He snapped back quickly. "You may be onto something, Coop. We'll undoubtedly get the warrant quickly, but getting a head start can't hurt. Stay professional, keep a low profile, and don't do anything that can hurt us later. Understand?" The lieutenant stepped toward him and aggressively placed his hand on his shoulder. A nervous grin emerged on Officer Cooper's face.

"Of course, yes, sir." He grabbed his jacket from the back of his chair and slowly made his way to the door.

"Riley, as for you, you're going to stay here until we get the warrant, and then-"

"Um, sir," Riley interrupted. "I have been stuck in these damp, dirty clothes for well over a day. I would love to go home and change, maybe take a quick shower, and check in on my cat. Could I step out for a bit? You said it yourself; we need to wait for the warrant to do anything further anyway!" Riley itched with optimism.

"Hmph," Lieutenant Nico sighed. "Cooper." He called out. Officer Cooper stopped just before shutting the door and turned to look back into the room. "Drop Riley off at her house and pick her up when you're done at the Hampton. Got it? I'll make sure the other officers know to keep an eye on her until you get back."

"I'm not under like...house arrest or anything, right?" Riley asked.

"No, absolutely not. But if there is any deviation and Kendra winds up at your house, I want to ensure you're protected."

Riley's stomach filled with warmth, like she'd just eaten a bowl of her mom's homemade soup.

"Thank you," Riley said softly as she vaulted from her chair to accompany Officer Cooper. They walked out of the room together and back toward the entrance she and the lieutenant had come through hours ago.

Little did the officers know that Riley did not intend to return to her house. She was on a war path of revenge, vengeance, and self-actualization. Now that she knew Kendra may be alive, she just had to convince Officer Cooper to follow her lead.

Officer Cooper opened the passenger side door for Riley. This was her first time riding shotgun next to an officer rather than behind them. She patiently waited for him to sit down in his seat before unveiling her ideas. He buckled the seatbelt and turned toward Riley.

"So, where are we headed?" He said with a slight smile.

Well, with a question like that, she guessed there was no time for small talk.

"The Hampton," Riley said bluntly with a cutesy smile across her face.

"Well, yeah, that's where I'm heading." Officer Cooper chuckled before pausing briefly. "But where am I dropping you off?" He asked again.

"I'd like to accompany you to the Hampton, Officer Cooper, sir." Riley sat up straight and folded her hands in her lap. Before saying a word, he quickly leaned forward to switch off his dash camera. He slowly faded back into his seat with his eyebrows slightly raised.

"First and foremost, you can call me Elija," Riley swore she saw a twinkle in his eye. "Secondly, there's no way in hell I can bring you with me. Nico would have my head on a stake before the end of the day. That's putting you in way too much danger. I just can't risk that. Not to mention, I would lose my job! I'm sorry. Tell me where your house is, and I'll drop you off there." Elija turned his body back toward the steering wheel.

A chill tickled Riley's body, sending goosebumps up her arms. *"Now is your time to be courageous. Stand up for yourself."* A shrill voice sounded in her head.

"Officer Nico said it himself. I'm not under house arrest. Right?"

220

Elija, looking puzzled, turned back toward Riley again. "Well, yeah, I guess so?"

"Annnnd the Hampton Inn is a public place of business, correct?"

"Alright, alright. I see where this is going. But I still can't be the one responsible for taking you there."

"Great! Drop me off a block away. At a random house a few streets down. Or anywhere within walking distance! They can't blame you for me giving you the wrong information," Riley said, blinking slowly, hoping to convince him to take the risk.

He gazed into her green eyes for what felt like minutes, contemplating morality. He shook his head as if an ice cube had dropped down his shirt.

"I'm sorry. I know you want to help. But I can't let you do this." His facial features drooped with disappointment. "Now, are you going to tell me where you live, or should I call the lieutenant?" Elija said reluctantly.

With a sigh, Riley uttered her street under her breath. "215 Sunnymeade Way."

"Ah, now we're talking." His voice lightened back to normal. "Away we go."

The car ride was awkwardly silent. The radio continually blared police codes until Elija clicked it off. He rolled down the driver's side window just a crack and pulled a pack of cigarettes from his pocket.

"Do you mind?" He asked.

"Your car, your rules!" Riley threw her hands in the air playfully. Even though she always had a repulsion to cigarette smoke and its carcinogenic properties.

Her mom, Lauri, used to smoke on occasion, only when she was extremely stressed. She tried to hide it from Riley, but the house always reeked of smoke when she returned. She still couldn't deny that smoking always made you look effortlessly relaxed, especially while wearing a police uniform.

"Do you smoke?" Elija asked Riley, offering the pack her way.

"No, no," she said. "I'm more of a gum chewer myself." Riley's cheeks immediately flushed with heat from her embarrassing remark. How childish could she be? Elija chuckled softly and put the pack back in his pocket.

"What kind?" He said, seemingly making small talk.

"Bubble-mint. Can't go wrong with bubble-mint." Riley peered out the window, awkwardly avoiding Elija's gaze.

"So," Elija said before taking a puff from his cancer stick. "Who were you before all of this? Before April...and Kendra. Before Clarendon Hills." The wind whisked away a plume of smoke as he exhaled his breath.

This bold question took Riley by complete surprise. "*How do I even begin to answer that?*" she questioned to herself, panicking for the right words to form in her brain.

"I was just an introverted girl from a desolate beach town." Words flowed like a waterfall from her mouth. Elija's calming energy reminded her of a blanket fresh out of the dryer. Talking to him felt like immersing yourself in a conversation with a friend you'd known your entire life.

"I was a writer. A pretty unsuccessful one, but still a writer. I really enjoyed listening to people talk and learning their stories. I was a peach iced tea junkie and had it with just about every meal; I still do, actually. I was my mom's best friend, and she was mine. We only had each other and hung onto that connection like glue." Riley paused for a moment, realizing the rabbit hole she was falling into. "I'm sorry, I don't know if that answered your question...I'm a bit awkwa-"

"Peach iced tea is my favorite, too!" He flashed a side smile. The tension in her shoulders melted into the chair behind her. She mustered up the courage to ask Elija the same question.

"So, what about...you?"

"Well, I've lived here all of my life. My grandfather was a lieutenant, so was my dad, and I guess you can see I'm following in their footsteps."

"Is that what you wanted to do?" Riley wondered if she overstepped.

Elija inhaled deeply, searching for the right words to say. "It's what I felt I needed to do. Uphold the family legacy, you know?"

"In a perfect world, what would you be doing instead?"

"Something with animals. I went to an aquarium with my dad when I was a kid. I couldn't have been any older than five or six. I walked up to the dolphin exhibit and swear to this day, the dolphin was trying to communicate with me. Kept opening his mouth and smiling at me. It was, clearly, an unforgettable experience." He said with a chuckle.

"There's still time," Riley said sincerely.

"There's still time for you to be a great writer, too." Elija retorted.

Endearment filled her chest. What started as an awkward car ride quickly morphed into a meaningful connection that she desperately needed.

As they slowly rolled into Riley's driveway, Elija clicked back on the dashboard camera and unlocked the doors. "I shouldn't be more than an hour. I'll be back to pick you up then. Hopefully, at that point, we'll have the warrant and clear evidence that Kendra is in the hotel. Then we'll get her once and for all."

Riley smiled through the frustration of not being able to go to the hotel herself. She nodded and stepped out of the car. Two other squad cars idled on the street in front of her house. Their tinted windows made it impossible to see who was inside.

Riley waved to Elija and ran toward her house. She jumped onto her porch steps, which let out a concerning creak. She leaned over and hesitantly lifted the turtle planter to find her spare key. With a sigh of relief, she was thankful that Kendra returned it the last time she used it. The door swung open, and Griddle immediately wrapped his body around her leg like a blanket. Just like her first day home from Triple C, she collapsed into a pool of emotion and smothered Griddle affectionately.

"I'm so sorry. I'm so sorry. I won't leave you like this again, I promise. I'm so sorry!" She repeated incessantly. She could feel his rib cage as she stroked his fur, making her wince. Darting to the kitchen, Griddle nuzzled his food bowl, which was completely empty. She was kicking herself for not filling his self-feeder to the brim. His water dish had mere drops left along the edge. After a quick refill, Griddle indulged. She sat down next to him as he filled his belly. Apologies and the sound of Griddle chewing were the only noises heard throughout their home.

She feared he'd be traumatized by her abandonment and that her absence would sever their bond. But thankfully, as soon as he got his fill, he nearly jumped into Riley's arms and refused to move, which gave her the indication that he forgave her once again.

She lifted herself and Griddle up from the floor and carried him into the bedroom. She plopped him down on her pillow, and he nestled down comfortably.

"Elija said he would be back in an hour. I guess I have time to take a quick shower." Griddle meowed in agreement. Riley waltzed into her bathroom and turned on the shower. A glimpse of herself in the mirror from the corner of her eye was enough to shock her. She leaned in closer, trying to recognize the person she saw. Her once bright orange hair had turned brassy. Her skin shimmered with oil and sweat. The whites of her eyes were nearly nonexistent, covered with popped blood vessels. Bruises cascaded over her arms and legs. Her clothes were wrinkled and damp. Riley felt another breakdown brewing. Not because she felt ugly but because the events over the past few days left her looking like a shell of herself, and she knew it wasn't over yet. She stared into her green eyes. The darkness of her pupils swallowed her whole.

"*You have to finish this, Riley.*" An indistinct voice rang in her head. "*This has to end with you.*"

"It's out of my control," she whispered to herself in the mirror.

"*Take it back. It could be hours before the officers do anything. Do you really trust them to finish the job?*" The voice pestered.

She wasn't sure if it was her conscience talking or just the sleep deprivation. Regardless, it made her thoughts swirl. The voice was right. With how lackadaisical and unorganized the officers were in the conference room, who knows how quickly they could find Kendra?

Riley knew she could be stealthier, faster, and apprehend her quicker. Nobody understood Kendra's mannerisms better than she did.

"*Go,* " the voice ordered. With that, Riley shut the water off and threw her hair into a quick ponytail. She walked swiftly back into her bedroom and frantically changed into dry clothes. An old baseball cap and sunglasses perfectly concealed her very noticeable hair and eye color.

"Shoot, my wallet and purse are still stuck at Kendra's house." Riley pouted in frustration—another hurdle in her way. An old black leather purse hung in her closet. It used to belong to her mom, and she never left the room without it. Yanking it from the hanger, she didn't bother to look inside. Griddle watched her every movement in awe, just thankful to be in her presence.

"Listen up, buddy. I promise I'll be back soon. Way sooner than before, okay?" Her hand stroked the back of his neck. He nuzzled her arm as she pulled away and ran back into the living room. She slipped on a pair of old shoes and grabbed the extra car key she had hanging on the hook by the door.

Her eyes clamped shut, and her lungs begged for a deep breath. Grabbing the door for balance, she allowed air to fill her nostrils before opening the door. She stopped in her tracks when the two idling officers were now outside of their cars, talking amongst themselves. When they heard the door open, they both immediately turned their attention to Riley.

"Going somewhere, Ms. Michaels?" One of the officers called.

"I, uh, I'm just running to the store. I'm out of a few things!" Riley called, slowly stepping off the porch.

"I'd be happy to go to the store for you! It'd be safer that way." He said, walking up the driveway.

Riley started to panic. "No, no! That won't be necessary! I, uh, need some special items. It's okay. I don't mind going." She chuckled, inching toward her car door.

"Just tell me what you need, and I'll-"

Riley cut off the officer. "Sir, I just started my period, and it's a HEAVY flow day. I need tampons. I'd really like to go get them myself if that's alright with you."

The officer's eyes grew to the size of dinner plates. "Er, yes. Yes ma'am. Carry on. Don't be too long," he grunted, walking backward down the driveway.

Riley smiled dotingly as she entered her car. As soon as she sat down, she rolled her eyes. "Men."

Fumbling to put the key in the ignition, she took another deep breath as she reversed away from her home. A sinking feeling hit the bottom of her stomach. Now that she was heading to The Hampton, she needed a plan. "*I can't just barge into her room and cuff her myself,*" Riley thought. There had to be a stealthier way of breaking in that didn't end with her back in jail.

As she entered the heart of the city, Riley could see the top of the Hampton above the other buildings. She ogled at the tall buildings as she cruised the streets. Coming from the middle of nowhere, she was still immensely impressed by the floors of concrete that filled the side streets.

As the hotel parking lot approached, she saw Elija's car up front near the valet, but he wasn't in the driver's seat. *"He must be inside."*

She parked on the side of the building, far back and next to a string of trees. Still, without a clear plan, she composed herself before grabbing her mom's purse, exiting her car, and walking toward the front entrance.

"Stay cool. Something will come to you. You've got this," she reassured herself as she was greeted by one of the valet drivers standing at the wooden podium.

"Good…afternoon?" The valet driver paused, eyeing Riley up and down. Even with the baseball cap, her matted hair poked through behind her ears. The largest sunglasses in the world couldn't conceal the grease caked on her face. The dark purple bruises on her wrists were a call for concern.

"Can't judge a book by its cover," Riley thought quietly as she nodded happily toward the driver.

The gold-plated revolving door swirled her into a warmly lit lobby with vaulted ceilings. A rounded desk lined the back of the room, and four concierges typed away at computers. Guests lounged on the furniture with their luggage by their side, waiting to be checked in and whisked up to their rooms.

Riley scanned the lobby until she saw Elija at the far end of the room talking with a security guard. They both had their arms crossed and were whispering quietly. Dipping the front of her baseball cap to hide her face, she turned around to find an open chair near the front window.

Her hands gravitated toward a slightly tattered magazine in front of her. She pretended to read it, subtly watching Elija's every move. She could feel the eyes of the valet driver staring at the back of her greasy head through the window. Her attention focused on the contents of the magazine. A large headshot of the singer P!nk was plastered on the front cover. Her hair was buzzed on the sides, and her eye makeup boasted a smoky blue hue that accentuated her eyes. As she flipped through, the articles discussed her rise to stardom, how she navigated being a mother, and her take on the music industry.

Riley's mom always loved listening to her songs. Anytime they came on the radio, she would say P!nk was one of the only female singers with "true talent." She always talked about how they went to the same high school. Riley wished she could hear her mom excitedly tell that random and embarrassing fact one more time.

She flipped through the pages and watched Elija follow the security guard to a back room behind the front desk. *"Finally,"* Riley uttered. Now was the perfect time to make her move. She slapped the magazine back down on the table and walked up to the concierge desk.

"Hi!" Riley's tone was more chipper than usual.

"Hello." The woman replied professionally.

"I'm not sure if you can help me. My sister and I are supposed to be having a girls' weekend, and she picked this beautiful hotel to stay at. Well, I left my phone at home, over two hours away, and can't remember the room number. I feel like such an idiot." Riley lathered on the theatrics by smacking her head. "This is going to ruin her birthday! Is there any way you could tell me what her room number is?" Riley flashed her best puppy dog eyes. She was impressed with her own performance.

"Ma'am, I'm sorry to hear that. But I can't give out another guest's personal information." Even the bluntness of her voice wouldn't make Riley stop trying. She carefully placed her hand on the counter.

"Of course! I understand; I don't want to put you in a difficult position."

"THINK!" The voice in her head screamed at her.

"But listen, I don't even know if I'm in the right place! I'm not from around here. Could you tell me if she's even staying at this hotel? I couldn't remember if it was this one or the one down the street. Ugh, I would lose my head if it wasn't attached!" Riley scoffed, silently hoping the concierge bought her story.

The woman let out a sigh. "Listen, this is against our protocol, but you seem pretty…desperate…" Her tone was filled with snark. "What's your sister's name?"

"Oh, thank you so much. This seriously means a lot to me. Her name is Kendra Fellowes." Riley's tongue burned at the taste of her name. The concierge typed feverishly into her computer and reviewed the files that populated.

"I'm sorry, I don't see her name in the system. She must not be staying here." She said, "If you'd like, you can use our phone in the computer room. It's right down the hall and to the left." She motioned.

"Wow, I guess I am in the wrong place. I appreciate your help. I think I'll try to give her a call. Thank you," she said, walking toward the hallway that she mentioned.

"Well, now what?" Riley stutter-stepped toward the computer room. Thankfully, Elija was still nowhere to be found.

Peeking into a small cubby-like room, there were three computers, a commercial-sized office printer, and a small table with a desk phone. She flopped down in the computer chair, spinning in circles, looking at the ceiling. The blinking red light on the smoke alarm seemed to match her frantic heart rate.

"*I'm running out of time. Elija is going to be heading to my house soon. I know Kendra is here. There's no reason Jared would lie about that. She must be using a fake name. And even if that's the case, this hotel has eight floors; I'd never find her in time.*"

Dark thoughts of Elija coming back to an empty house loomed in her brain. "*Maybe I should just go back and let them handle it.*" Her thoughts whirled from swirling in the chair. As she spun, her mom's black leather purse slid from her shoulder, and the contents spilled across the floor.

She rolled the chair backward to grab everything from under the table. She hadn't looked through this purse since her mom passed away. Her favorite citrus medicated Chapstick, the black ballpoint pen she insisted on using over any other, the stacks and stacks of salad-shop coupons, a translucent orange lighter with just a few drops of fluid left, and a lone red-and-white box of cigarettes, with two sticks remaining inside. She chuckled, knowing her mom was an unapologetic health nut who still couldn't kick the habit.

"*Riley, FOCUS!*" The familiar internal voice yelled.

She lay her head back on the chair to stare at the ceiling again. The blinking red light taunted her until suddenly, it became the lightbulb above her head. She fished the lighter from the purse again and held both the cigarette box and the lighter in her hands.

"If I can't find you...I'm going to make you come to me."

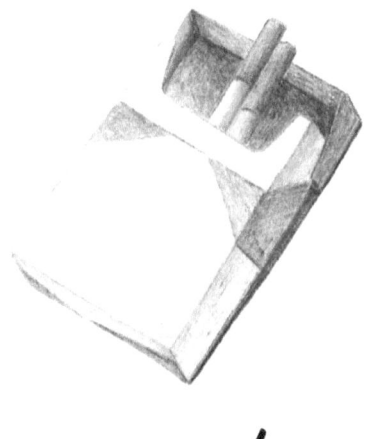

evacuation

Even from a young age, Riley had always been sure of herself. She didn't wait for anyone's permission to get what she wanted - she just went for it. Once she realized she could force Kendra into her presence by evacuating the hotel, nothing was going to stop her, even the thought of catching a felony. In Riley's mind, April's safety meant more than hers. She could live out her sentence as a hero instead of wishing she could have done more.

After flicking the box open again, it revealed the last two cigarettes left by her mom. She slowly slid a stick from the carton and held it in front of her face. Her sweaty fingers gripped the lighter and clicked the ignition. A bright blue and orange flame emerged from the sparks. Riley inhaled deeply, hoping that her plan worked and worked quickly.

She joined the cigarette and the lighter together, and the stick immediately began to burn. The smoke billowed and rose to the ceiling. She looked outside of the computer room to check if the coast was clear before jumping up on the table in front of her. Her arm extended high above her head, hoping the smoke would reach the alarm faster. Within seconds, a screeching noise blared through every room.

Riley quickly dropped the cigarette on the table and smashed it with her foot. She leaped from the edge, mildly straining her ankles, before booking it out of the room. She slowed to a power walk as she reentered the lobby. Her eyes glanced toward the front desk and noticed the two cops who were sitting outside of her house were suddenly scoping out the lobby. Realizing they must have followed her, she panicked, lowering her hat to cover her face even more. She quickly blended into the sea of scared hotel guests.

"Everyone, please make your way to the front entrance. We need to evacuate immediately. This is not a drill!" one of the concierges called.

"Yes!" Riley victoriously whispered, slipping her hands in her pockets and walking toward the door. As she stepped, she nearly locked eyes with Elija, who walked up to the edge of the check-in desk to speak with the other officers. Her hand raised, and she immediately pushed the sunglasses up the bridge of her nose to shield her eyes.

Everyone filtered into the valet area, pushing and shoving as more guests fled. Riley turned toward the door, hoping to spot Kendra as she walked out, but all the faces were unfamiliar. Two fire trucks raced into the parking lot within minutes, and men poured from the doors.

"I NEED EVERYONE AT LEAST 100 FEET FROM THIS BUILDING IMMEDIATELY. FOLLOW ME PLEASE." The firefighter called, motioning everyone farther away from the building.

"*Seriously?*" Riley questioned as she side-stepped. Her eyes scanned the crowd of bobbing heads, anticipating spotting Kendra from the masses, but she had no luck.

"*Maybe this was a bad idea...*" Riley's anxiety surged.

"OKAY, THIS IS FAR ENOUGH. WAIT HERE UNTIL WE GIVE THE ALL-CLEAR TO RETURN TO THE BUILDING. WE APPRECIATE YOUR PATIENCE." The firefighter yelled.

Riley stood on her tiptoes to look over the crowd. People were continually shuffling toward the "safe zone." The indistinct chatter broke Riley's concentration. She must have stared down every white woman with short brown hair, and still no Kendra.

"Maybe Jared was wrong. Maybe I was wrong." Feeling dejected, she pushed her way through the crowd in search of a pathway back to her car.

"I better get out of here before Elija heads back to the house to get me."

The sea of people parted, and one woman stood out among the rest. She was short, with freshly bleached blonde hair, and was wearing sunglasses and a dark-colored hoodie. Her mannerisms were peculiar—she constantly looked from left to right and held her hands nervously.

Riley stood observing the woman for a moment as people shoved her from side to side. A large man with a rolling suitcase bumped into the woman, causing her sunglasses to fall. She quickly bent down to pick them up, but before she could conceal her eyes again, Riley got a glimpse at what had been hiding underneath.

"Those…those are Kendra's eyes. Kendra's fucking eyes." Riley roared. Kendra turned toward the parking lot without seeing Riley and walked away from the crowd.

"*This is your moment, Riley. RUN!*" The voice in her head yelled. Riley sprinted toward Kendra, disregarding anyone in her way.

"Watch it, lady!" One man said.

"Hey! Where are you running off to?" A woman called. Riley couldn't hear anything but the sound of her panting breath exhaling from her lungs. Her feet shook the pavement like miniature earthquakes. The breeze from her sprint made her baseball cap fly off.

"Ms., you forgot this!" Another man called. Kendra must have heard him speak because she turned around to see if he was talking to her. She quickly realized Riley was right behind her.

Without care for her landing, Riley tackled Kendra to the ground like she was a star linebacker. Kendra let out a shriek as her shoulder and collarbone collided with the ground. Straddling Kendra, Riley turned her over to get a glimpse of her face. She lowered her body onto hers, inches away from Kendra's ear.

"Gotcha." Riley snickered. The screams and howls of bystanders yelling for help were merely faint background noise to this glorious and heroic moment for Riley.

"The cops will be here any second. I've got her." Riley thought confidently.

Kendra stared into Riley's green eyes for only a moment before throwing a punch directly into her jaw. Riley wailed in pain as blood dripped out of her mouth and down her chin. Fueled with adrenaline and rage, Riley sent a blow to Kendra's face, then another, then another.

Through her wailing, she screamed, "SOMEONE GET THE POLICE," as blood pooled in her mouth. Various voices begged for her to stop, and within seconds, two officers surrounded the scene. Kendra was nearly unconscious from the beating. Her face swelled like a wasp had injected her with venom. Riley's mouth continued to bleed down the front of her shirt.

"HANDS WHERE I CAN SEE THEM!" The officer demanded. Thinking he was just talking about Kendra, Riley rolled off of her. She stood up to let the officer cuff her once and for all. One officer looked at Riley with fire in his eyes.

"I SAID HANDS WHERE I CAN SEE THEM. I WON'T ASK AGAIN!"

"Me? Do you mean her? She's the criminal, not me!" Riley pleaded before being aggressively handcuffed, reopening the fragile wounds that circled her wrists from the night before. The other officer cuffed Kendra and hoisted her limp body up on her feet. They slowly walked toward the parked police cars. Riley and her officer followed.

"You going to tell me what the hell that was?" The officer asked Riley.

"Justice," she responded without thinking. Her eyes widened after the last syllable left her tongue.

"What did you just say?" He asked.

"Do you know who I am?" Riley asked confidently.

"Should I?"

"Sir, I don't want to have to plead the fifth, but I need to speak with Lieutenant Nico immediately."

"You don't get to make the rules around here, sweetheart. That's why you're in cuffs, and I'm the one escorting you. Sit down, shut up, and I'll deal with you after I make sure this fire is under control." He shoved her head in the back of the police car. She watched as Kendra was placed in the back of the other car, and she immediately slumped over on her side.

———

Riley sat alone in the back of the car with only her thoughts to occupy her. She watched each minute tick away on the car radio. Still in restraints, she couldn't wipe the blood from her chin. She had to helplessly watch each drop seep into the fibers of her pants. She stared blankly into the rear-view mirror, watching the crowd of people shuffle back into the hotel.

"How did I end up here again?" Riley asked into the void of the silent car. "After they threw me in jail for weeks? After uncovering a mystery that they couldn't solve? After everything I had done for them. How I advocated for April and myself. This is the thanks I get? A cracked jaw and bloody wrists from the handcuffs being too tight? This is BULLSHI-" She was interrupted by the door swinging open. Light poured into the car, blinding Riley for a moment before she recognized the face in front of her.

"Thank god, can you get me-" Riley was cut off again.

"What were you thinking?" Lieutenant Nico barked. "You know, it's not often that someone gets off scot-free from faking a fire, let alone in a hotel. Are you insane?" He slapped the roof of the car violently.

"How...how did you know that was me?" Riley asked nervously. He quickly held up his phone to reveal the security camera footage of Riley on the table in the computer room. She quickly looked away from the phone.

"I did what I thought I had to do. This started with me, and I wanted to be the one to end it." She said slowly, waiting for an explosion.

"Now is not the time for a god complex, Riley! We had the warrant at our fingertips! All you had to do was wait." He paced back and forth in front of the car door, fuming with frustration. "You know that this could be considered a felony, Riley. This is serious. And I heard you beat the crap out of her, too?" His fingers rubbed his temples, unsure of what else to say.

Forgetting she was still handcuffed, Riley tried to put a finger up to stop him. "Don't get this twisted. She threw the first punch." The man let out a large sigh as he put his hand on the car door. He focused his attention on the other car and watched Kendra sway back and forth in her seat. He made eye contact with Riley again.

"Through all of this, I need to personally acknowledge what she," he paused, " and we as a department put you through." Riley didn't think this situation could get any more puzzling. *"Was that an apology?"* She thought. She was too stunned to speak.

"PANELLA." He called across the parking lot. "Take her back to the station and put her in a holding cell. I'll follow you with Kendra." His eyes met Riley's for the last time.

"This isn't over, and I'm not done with you yet. We'll talk at the station," he said, slamming the door.

Officer Panella jumped in the front seat and flicked on his lights and sirens. They sped away from the Hampton, leaving Riley more nervous than when she arrived.

———

Riley's arms twitched with pain as Officer Panella pulled her from the back seat. "Hate to do this to you, kid. But you made some incredibly poor choices today."

"Did I?" Riley questioned in her head. *"Or are you frustrated that I did your job for you?"* She shook her head to clear her mind of the narcissistic thoughts.

Officer Panella walked her into the building through the lobby with the fishbowl glass counter and led them down a hallway. His badge triggered the door to open to a room filled with metal bars. Panella took a deep breath.

"In you go, Ms. Michaels." He guided her into one of the cells, released her handcuffs, and shut the door.

"How long is he going to keep me locked up in here?" Riley rubbed her wrists, which were covered in dark red scrapes.

"Nico didn't say. He'll be here soon and will come talk to you." He released his grip from the bars and walked out of the room. Riley was alone again, trapped in an eight-foot concrete room with a rotting wooden bench and a metal toilet.

"This is how little they think of me," she said, plopping down on the bench. By the way it creaked, she feared it wouldn't hold her weight for long. She looked past the bars to the other holding cells across the room. Both were empty. Her watery eyes came back to center. Her head tensed with frustration, and her veins pulsated violently.

"I found Kendra. How could they do this to me?" She yelled with anger, blind to the massive scene she had caused back at the hotel. She closed her eyes in an attempt to stop her streaking tears. Her mind relaxed as April's toothy grin flashed in her mind.

Riley jolted from her daze at the sound of rattling metal. Lieutenant Nico stood in front of the bars, repeatedly hitting his handcuffs on the holding cell to wake her up.

"Sir." Her tone exuded grogginess.

"I think you earned this."

"Earned...what?"

Lieutenant Nico fumbled with his keys before opening her cell. He motioned her to follow him, which she did promptly. She wasn't sure where he was taking her, but if she had to smell the foul ammonia coming from the toilet in her cell any longer, she was going to vomit.

He walked her down another set of never-ending hallways without saying a word. She followed blindly, hoping this wasn't a trap. Another right and another left led them to an inconspicuous door labeled "489". Lieutenant Nico shuffled Riley in.

As her eyes adjusted, she saw a dark room with a few dimly lit computer screens along the back wall. In front of her was a large two-way mirror. Lieutenant Nico greeted Officer Panella, hiding in the back corner of the room. The two small-talked as Riley crept closer toward the mirror.

Through the glass, she saw a familiar room with dented walls and a porcelain-tiled floor. A wooden table stood in the middle of the room, and at the table sat Kendra with her arms crossed and her leg chained to the chair. Her face was almost completely purple from the bruises. Dark, dried blood seeped from every orifice. Riley shuddered, knowing she was the culprit behind her appearance, but quickly settled, knowing nobody in the world was more deserving than her. Riley looked back at the lieutenant.

"What am I doing here?" She cautiously looked through the mirror again.

"No questions. Just watch." He pulled up a chair for Riley to sit in. She sat in the uncomfortably cold metal chair that sent a shiver up her spine. She stared ominously at Kendra.

"I can't believe they have her. They really have her!"

Riley's body jolted as Elija came through the door on the opposite side of the mirror. Kendra quickly looked back to see who it was and winced at the sight of another officer.

"Kendra Fellowes, is it? Or are you going by Lauri Michaels now? Did you have a nice stay at the Hampton?"

Riley gripped the edge of her seat. Goosebumps created tiny mountains across her skin.

"Why…why would she use my mom's name to check into the hotel? What a full-blown psychopath." Riley scoffed out loud. She quickly covered her mouth and looked back at Lieutenant Nico.

"Don't worry. She can't hear you," he reassured her. She breathed a sigh of relief and went back to watching the interrogation.

"It's Kendra," she said, emotionless. Elija sat down in front of her. "Why am I here? I did nothing wrong." Kendra spat blood droplets on the table as she talked.

"I didn't say you did anything wrong. I simply asked your name, Mrs. Fellowes. You have a fairly clean record. The only document in your file states that you filed a missing person report nearly a month ago. Is that true?"

"Yes."

"And this was for your...dau..."

"My daughter. It was for my daughter. And don't think I forgot how little you all did to find her either."

"I can't speak for the rest of my team, but after reading your file, I personally want to invest all my time into finding your little girl. That's partially why you're here. I'm sure you must be worried sick about her. Can you tell me a bit about her? Maybe the place you last saw her? Anything you can give us would be helpful." Elija seemed genuinely concerned.

"If you look in that pretty little file of yours, it should have everything from my initial report listed," Kendra said in a snarky tone, folding her arms across her body.

"Well, Mrs. Fellowes. I'm sorry, is it Miss? Is there a mister?" Elija asked. A bead of sweat formed on the side of Kendra's head that dripped down to her shirt.

"Ew, are you coming onto me? Of course, I had-" Kendra forced a cough from her throat to cover up her statement. "Excuse me. Of course, I have a husband."

"Ma'am, I was merely asking if I should be using Mrs. or Ms., that's all. Thank you for clarifying. Now, in your report, you mentioned your babysitter, nanny...which is it?" He asked.

"Why are you asking me the most ridiculous questions? Can you please get to the point of all of this? Why am I really here?"

Kendra's voice was angry. Her ankles shook and rattled the chains around them.

"I am trying to ensure I have all of the facts to help you find your daughter, Kendra."

"You're right." Kendra composed herself. "She was our nanny. Her name was Riley."

Riley's ears perked up at the sound of her name.

"Riley…Last name?"

Kendra began to stutter, knowing she had stolen Riley's last name as her alias.

"M…Michaelson? M…McCormick? M…Maverick? Sir, I don't remember."

"You hired Riley to be your nanny without knowing her last name?"

"Uh…oh! Now I remember…her last name is Michaels. Like the arts and crafts store."

"Oh yeah, my niece loves that place! She's only three, but she loves picking up packs of stickers and markers. Her name is Lauren. Was your daughter into crafting?"

Kendra gulped at the sound of Lauren's name. "N…no, no, not yet. She's coming up on her second birthday. It's hard t-to even believe it," Kendra said, smiling nervously.

"Are you doing okay? I know this must be emotional to talk about."

"Yes. Yes. I'm fine. I would just really like to go home. I don't belong here."

"Just a few more questions, and you'll be on your way. So, back to this nanny you hired, Riley Michaels. She's young, old?"

"Young, like you," Kendra observed his youthfulness.

"I'm flattered, Mrs. Fellowes. So, it says here that she, and let me make sure I have this right, put your daughter in the wrong car? And whoever was driving sped off with your daughter? Can you detail that a bit more?" Elija asked, pulling a pen from his pocket to "take notes."

"Well, there isn't much more to tell. My husband called me and said he couldn't pick up our daughter due to a work conflict. I texted Riley and said I would pick her up myself. From what Riley said, she never saw my message, and someone matching my husband's description arrived at her house. She put April in the car, and off they went. I haven't seen her since. If you want my honest opinion, I think Riley was in on it the whole time. I don't have a motive yet, but I know she was behind it all."

"Do you know who the driver could have been? Maybe a disgruntled family member or friend?" Elija asked.

"Nope. No idea."

"Hm, okay. So, you obviously called the police, and Riley got taken away. Have you talked to her since?" He asked, pretending to write notes feverishly. Kendra paused for a moment, longer than she should have.

"Riley? No."

"That dirty liar!" Riley muttered.

"For all I know, she's still in jail. Where she belongs." Kendra crossed her arms.

"If what you're telling me is true, she definitely deserves to do her time," Elija assured, projecting pseudo-empathy to Kendra. "Now, your husband. Where is he?" Elija asked.

"Hell, if I know," Kendra said abruptly before faking another cough. "It's just...he works too much. He's a traveling pharmacist, so I never truly know where he is."

"But with your daughter missing? Surely, he must be worried sick. I'm surprised he's able to focus on anything else."

"You and I both," she said, avoiding his gaze. Elija let the statement go.

"Let's get down to the basics. Why are you here today, Mrs. Fellowes? Well, my partners separated you from a pretty nasty fight earlier at the Hampton. Do you want to tell me what happened there?"

"I wish I could. I have no idea. One minute we're evacuating the hotel from a fire or something, and the next, I am getting pummeled by that bitch."

"'That...bitch?' You know who she was?"

"No, no, you must have misheard me. I said some bitch. Excuse my language."

"Got it. It sounds like there are a lot of unknowns in your story. Your daughter is missing, kidnapped by someone completely random, and now you're getting mauled by strangers in broad daylight? Are you part of the mob and not telling me?" Elija cracked a joke to break the tension.

"I wish I were. I feel like I'd get answers a lot quicker that way." Kendra stared blankly at the two-way mirror. Terrified that she could see through, Riley looked away briefly.

"Oh, why were you staying in a hotel anyway? Your file says you live just a short drive from there." Elija asked, starting to dig in.

"Yeah, well, I had to have the pest control guys come bomb my house. Fleas...couldn't get rid of the fleas. Such a problem this time of year."

"Shew, I know the pain when it comes to bugs. My dog Travis loves to roll around in the bushes. He comes home covered in fleas and ticks!" Kendra's left eye twitched. "That still doesn't explain why you decided to use an alias at check-in. Just felt like being someone new for the day?" Elija asked.

Kendra shrugged her shoulders and refused to speak. She knew he was onto her facade.

"When did you check into the hotel?"

"Two days ago." She surprisingly complied.

"Did you stop anywhere before checking in?"

"No."

The room fell silent. Elija closed the folder he was holding and looked directly into Kendra's eyes. She stared back at him with confusion.

"I have an alibi that says otherwise, Mrs. Fellowes."

"Oh, do you?" Kendra's previously emotionless expression showed very obvious cracks. Her lip twitched in sync with her eye.

"GET HER, ELIJA!" Riley spoke.

"I do. The hundreds of fingerprints you left in Travis Hoffman's home after you brutally murdered him."

Kendra looked through Elija blankly, like someone had dropped an atomic bomb on her head.

"I don't know what you're talking about." She said coldly. You could almost see the ice shards escaping her mouth with each word she spoke.

"Did you know Travis, Kendra?" Elija asked.

"I don't know what you're talking about," she repeated.

"He had the sweetest pictures of April on his walls. This had to have been someone who knew you and your daughter well, right?"

Kendra remained silent, clenching her fists until her knuckles were white.

"I'm surprised she hasn't asked for a lawyer. When is she going to crack?" Riley sat on the edge of her seat.

"Me too, but just wait for it." Lieutenant Nico called.

"But you want to know the strangest part? When we searched his home, we stumbled into a little girl's room, with a sign on the wall that read Laur...."

"Her name is APRIL," Kendra shouted, slamming her fists on the table.

"Are you sure about that? Or is that what you changed it to when you took her?"

"YOU DON'T UNDERSTAND. SHE WAS MEANT TO BE WITH ME. SHE WAS MEANT TO BE MY DAUGHTER." Every ounce of Kendra's body thrashed uncontrollably. "MY DAUGHTER. MY DAUGHTER. MY DAUGHTER. WHERE IS MY DAUGHTER?!" Kendra screamed at the top of her lungs.

"I'm going to give you a minute to calm down. I'll be back." Elija walked into the back room where Riley was. She scooted her chair away from the door to avoid catching Kendra's gaze. Elija was stunned to see Riley, but he immediately turned his attention to Lieutenant Nico.

"Great work, Cooper. Just like your old man." He said, patting his shoulder. Riley watched Kendra wail in her seat, nearly knocking over the table in the center of the room. It was a bad car accident; you just couldn't look away from it.

"Riley," Lieutenant Nico said. She rose from her chair. "Remember I said I wasn't finished with you? Follow me. I think we've all seen enough here."

"Yes, sir," Riley said, making subtle eye contact with Elija before following the lieutenant.

Riley recounted the interrogation as she walked. Euphoria rushed over her body like a tidal wave—a confession. A conviction is on the horizon. Finally, a sense of relief knowing April was no longer in any danger. Because of that, Riley didn't care what happened next. Lieutenant Nico led them into a room identical to the one she watched Kendra confess in. They both sat down. Riley felt the need to break the silence.

"I appreciate you for letting me witness that. I'm thankful knowing that April is going to be safe."

"This isn't over yet."

"What? What do you mean? You got a confession!"

Lieutenant Nico became increasingly frustrated with Riley's lack of understanding of how serious the situation was.

"With everything you did back at the Hampton? Riley, you should be heading off to jail right behind Kendra!"

"Everything I did?" Riley questioned. "What about everything you did to me? You completely used me for information without any recognition, appreciation, or sense of security. You made me feel like I was walking on eggshells for the past two days." She paused to collect her thoughts.

"Oh, and let us not forget that I was wrongfully in jail by your department. I would still be in there if it weren't for Ms. Jane Doe bailing me out. Who, news flash, was actually KENDRA! At this point, I have more to thank her for than you! Do you realize how messed up that sounds?" The veins bulged from Riley's arms. Her body fumed with fire.

"You don't think I realize all of that?" The lieutenant yelled. "That's why I busted my ass to make sure you didn't end up in the state prison! You thought County Jail was bad? Boy, you wouldn't be able to handle the stories I could tell you." He chuckled angrily. Riley reclused.

"Listen up and listen good." The lieutenant pushed his thumb and index finger together until they were just barely touching. "You were this close to going back today, and I mean that. You're lucky I have a great rapport with our Chief of Police, or you would've been bunkies with Kendra within minutes."

Riley faded back into her chair as her eyes glossed. Lieutenant Nico grew tired of lecturing Riley. "I'm going to have Panella take you home. You are not to leave your house for any reason, understand? And stay the hell away from the hotel. We may have a lawsuit on our hands because of you." He said, shooing her away as he opened the door to exit.

Riley refused to move from her chair. There was still unfinished business.

"Come on." Lieutenant Nico called, increasing his frustration levels.

"Amari," Riley said, crossing her arms.

"Psh, c'mon, Riley. I don't have time for this."

"You do. Because you know who is wrongfully losing their time? Amari." She stood firm.

"Wrongfully!?" The lieutenant yelled, slamming the door and reentering the room. "WRONGFULLY!?" He yelled again. "She pulled a gun on a man…in his own house!" He said, slamming his hands on the table. Riley stood to match his stance.

"You mean the same man that Kendra MURDERED? Just because he was Lauren's FATHER?" Riley slammed her hands on the table. "He wasn't even there that night!" Riley poured. "The victim is DEAD, Lieutenant. And you know just as well as I do that if your kid went missing, there is NOTHING you wouldn't do to find them." Riley walked past him to open the door. His face was perplexed. She could practically see the cogs in his brain spinning.

"I'm not promising anything." He followed Riley out of the room.

875222

Riley anxiously awaited a police car to roll up her driveway. Her footsteps paced every inch of her living room, and Griddle followed closely behind.

"I'm sorry; I know I'm freaking you out. I'M freaking out." Nuzzling him calmed her briefly. After plopping on the couch, her arms wrapped around her throw pillow. Freshly washed and straightened hair danced between her fingers. Her gardenia perfume's sweet and subtle aroma made Riley radiate freshness and confidence, feelings that seemed distant after the past few weeks.

Just then, she heard an abrupt knock at the door. Though prepared for a visitor, she still jumped from the noise. She quickly shuffled through the living room to open the door. There stood Elija, the first time they had been alone since yesterday's interrogation. He gazed at her in disbelief, hardly recognizing her newly polished appearance. She instinctively lunged into his arms, crushing his walkie-talkie and body camera into her chest. He wrapped his arms around Riley and squeezed gently.

"I don't even know what to say. You...you got her to confess! This is all over because of you!" Riley spilled frantically before being cut off by Elija's calming voice.

"You don't have to thank me. I was just doing my job." He reluctantly unlinked his arms from around her back. They both stood under Riley's doorway, awkwardly gawking at each other. Eagerly anticipating the day, she broke the tension. "So, should we go?"

"Oh yeah, yes! Of course."

Riley patted Griddle on the head before walking out the door. "I'll be back. I extra super promise this time."

She locked the door behind her and followed Elija to his squad car. He ran to the passenger side door to open it for Riley. Appreciating his generosity, she thanked him before sitting on the leather seat.

Elija quickly entered the driver's side and buckled up. Dust plumed behind the car as it retreated down the driveway. A thrill snaked through Riley, not of fear but of anticipation. She began to fixate on the only thing that mattered.

"So…" Riley said. "What's the plan for today?"

"You know, I'm not entirely sure," he said genuinely. "Nico hasn't told me much. He seemed pretty heated yesterday, so I didn't bother asking questions. You must have really struck a nerve."

Riley swallowed the lump in her throat. "Oh, okay." She said, filling the car with silence again. She could feel her lips quivering, wanting to ask more. "But, do you know if I'm going to be able to see April?" Hope beamed with every word she spoke.

"If I knew more, I'd tell you!" He responded playfully.

A determined smile stretched across Riley's face. Since Lieutenant Nico practically granted her immunity yesterday, the weight on her chest had dissipated. Each shallow breath she took fueled her anticipation. The police station loomed only twenty minutes away, so she gazed out the window to pass the time. Riley followed the power lines and tried forming shapes with the clouds.

"Being home had to feel pretty nice, huh?" Elija glanced toward Riley. Caught off guard by his casual question, she met his gaze and chuckled.

"I bathed for the first time in days, gorged myself on pizza, and passed out on the couch. I'd say it was a perfect first night back."

"Hey!" Elija exclaimed. "I had pizza last night too! What a small world."

"Alright," Riley said quickly, shifting her weight to look at her new pal. "Pineapple on pizza...yay or nay." She questioned whimsically.

"Oh, gross! You're not one of those people, are you?" A scowl stretched across his face.

"I'm disappointed to inform you that I am one of those people. Do you want me to just jump out now?" She said, placing her hand on the door handle.

"No, no, no... no, pizza is worth jumping out of a moving vehicle for." He quickly claimed defeat.

"I don't know, if I saw a deep-dish pineapple pizza out the window right now, I might have some serious thoughts about jumping ship!"

The pair's laughter slowly faded into a simple conversation about their favorite movies, bands, and colors. Though Riley wasn't the best at making friends, especially since moving to Illinois, she felt like talking to Elija was effortless.

Riley had craved surface-level, light-hearted questions after the intensity she faced over the past few days. Her heart fluttered with excitement with each word he spoke. Annoyingly, her internal monologue interrupted her carefree conversations.

"*Stay focused on April,*" her brain repeated.

Reality barged back into view. Riley shifted her body back and focused on staring out the window. The car filled with silence once again.

The next few minutes passed with warp speed as Riley daydreamed of April being in her arms again. Elija pulled into the station and shifted the car into park. Riley attempted to open the door, but the handle wouldn't budge. She heard Elija snickering as he unlocked the door.

"See, you couldn't have jumped out for that pizza even if you wanted to!" Elija smirked. Riley laughed as she unlatched her seatbelt and followed him inside the building.

The pair moved quickly past the door they used yesterday. Riley pondered what building Elija could be taking her to. They walked along a narrow sidewalk lined with blooming pink petunias. The path is connected to a building attached to the main station. He motioned Riley to the side door and gripped the cold, metal handle.

"Hey, remember when I said I didn't know anything?" Elija shrugged, avoiding eye contact.

Riley looked at him with confusion. "Yeah?"

"Well, that may have been a little white lie." He opened the door, and there, standing in the middle of the bleak hallway, was Lieutenant Nico holding the most beautiful, bubbly, curly-haired little girl.

Riley tripped over her own feet to run inside. "APRIL!" She screamed, snatching the girl from his arms. Riley buried her face in April's neck.

"Ry Ry," she yelled, squeezing Riley's arms. She looked deeply into her eyes.

"Are you okay?" Riley asked.

"Yep!" April was as excited as ever. "Ry Ry!" She repeated. April's tiny hand lay perfectly on Riley's shoulder. With a playful scowl, Riley locked eyes with Elija, who was in on it the entire time. Her gaze then shifted back to Lieutenant Nico.

"Thank you." She expressed endearingly.

"Well, don't thank me yet. We've got one more…surprise for you."

"Sir, with all due respect, I don't think I can handle any more surprises. This is plenty for me."

"Just follow me." He said, walking down the hallway. She and Elija quickly caught up to him. "Let's talk in my office for a minute. Elija, would you mind going to meet up with the others? They're working on the press conference materials for today."

"Oh, yes. Sure. Of course!" His voice cracked awkwardly as he continued down the hallway past Lieutenant Nico's office. As Riley watched him inch farther away, she felt like her security blanket was being ripped away. After breathing deeply, she stepped into the lieutenant's office.

Riley sat on one of the plastic chairs in front of his desk. April took an interest in the assortment of rainbow highlighters he had resting in his pen cup. He quickly grabbed a sheet of paper from the printer so April could doodle. Riley sat her in the chair next to hers and focused her attention on Lieutenant Nico.

"Here, I think these belong to you." The lieutenant plopped her purse and phone on the desk. Riley snatched them up quickly. "Found them at Kendra's place."

"Thank you!" Riley gushed, putting them off to the side.

"So, things got pretty tense between you and me last night." He said matter-of-factly.

"Uh," Riley began. "Yeah, I'd say so."

"In any other circumstance, we would have carried you back to Clarendon Correctional, but...what we put you through is nothing short of horrendous. And because of that, I have a proposition for you."

"Oh, do you?" Her intrigue deepened by his statement. The lieutenant leaned forward in his squeaky chair.

"What do you say we call a truce?" He questioned.

"You're going to have to give me more than that. What's included in this truce?"

"You shake my hand, and the relationship we have will be wiped clean. I'm admitting our wrongdoings as a department, and I urge you to do the same." His hand stuck toward Riley.

"There's no paperwork to sign? Just...a handshake?" She scoffed, trying to comprehend the legitimacy of his offer.

"Just a handshake and a whole lot of trust. I've been up all night putting the legal puzzle together." He winked.

Riley thought for a moment, then immediately grabbed his hand. Her force shook the table, knocking over April's pen cup.

"Truce."

"Truce." He agreed, gripping her hand firmly. Riley smiled. Her name was finally done being dragged through the mud. She looked down at April, who happily took the caps off the highlighters just to put them back on.

"Has anyone contacted Amari?" Riley questioned.

"Well, yes and no." Lieutenant Nico said, avoiding her gaze.

"Well, what does that mean?"

"In about 30 minutes, Amari is going to be taken to an interrogation room, where you will meet her with April."

Riley's eyes widened.

"You want me to tell her that she...uh...are you sure?"

"You said you wanted to be the hero, Ms. Michaels. Now's your time to be one." A smirk escaped the corner of his lips.

Emotions swirled in her head and flowed right out of her mouth. "How am I even supposed to tell her? Where do I start? I haven't spoken to her in days!" Panic set in. "What if she hates me? What if she thinks I've been associated with her daughter's kidnappers this whole time?"

"Riley, all that matters is that you found her. As soon as you walk in there with that little girl, she'll just know."

Riley pondered for a minute, watching April's hair bounce with each scribble. "Does... this mean you're shortening her sentence?" Her pitch rose with each word.

"Let's focus on one thing at a time." He responded, typing something into his computer. After another few seconds of silence, Riley confidently responded.

"Okay. I'm in. Which car are we taking?"

———

Once again, Riley and April sat uncomfortably in the back of a police car, hopefully for the last time. Riley held April's hand as her little fingers played with the seat belt buckle. Lieutenant Nico switched back and forth between talking on his walkie-talkie and calling people on his phone. It was a non-stop conversation.

From what Riley gathered, the locals were starting to question the timeline of events and how the department didn't pick up on the connection sooner. Apparently, Lieutenant Nico would be hosting a press conference to set the record straight and inform the public that little Miss Lauren Syke had been found safe seven months after her initial kidnapping. Riley's name came up frequently in his chats, but with only hearing one side of the discussion, her head filled with questions.

In what felt like only a few short minutes, the car arrived in the parking lot of Triple C. Riley's arms and legs prickled with goosebumps, and a shiver lingered down her spine. Seeing the beige concrete walls and barbed wire fences made her wince. She held onto April's hand tightly for support.

They pulled the car around to the officer's lot, and Lieutenant Nico promptly unlocked the doors. Riley unbuckled April and carried her over her shoulder. She adjusted April's shirt, which displayed pink and orange tie-dye swirls that said, "Today's A Good Day." Riley smiled, knowing that her shirt was finally telling the truth.

April's body was held close to hers as they followed behind Lieutenant Nico. They walked through a large set of double doors into the same lobby where Riley patiently sat before being released less than a week ago.

The pungent smell of the floor polish was a slap in the face, reopening her actively healing wound. Memories of being behind these very walls flooded her mind. She quickly shook her head like an Etch-A-Sketch to erase her thoughts.

Lieutenant Nico leaned into the glass pane separating him from the front guard. "Here to see 875222, Syke. You should've gotten a call."

"Yeah, you're good to go," he said, opening the door to enter the jail. The front guard came around from his seat to pat down Lieutenant Nico, then Riley, then April. She squirmed in Riley's arms, scared that the man was going to take her away from Riley again.

"Shhh, it's ok! Just a couple of tickles," Riley assured her. The guard gave the all-clear, and Lieutenant Nico led Riley down a pathway to yet another building.

"*Stay focused,*" Riley repeated in her head, trying to avoid her surroundings.

As they entered the building, they took a sharp left down an unmarked hallway. Another right and another left led them to a door. Lieutenant Nico shuffled the girls in. Two unfamiliar officers greeted them. Riley experienced a severe case of Deja Vu walking into the same back-end interrogation room as yesterday. Instead of Kendra sitting in the middle of the concrete room, it was Amari.

Riley's eyes glistened at the sight of her friend, in disbelief that she was on the other side of the wall. She stared at Amari for a few moments, observing her mannerisms and noticeable wardrobe changes. No longer was she covered in bright orange; her body was cloaked in baggy gray sweats. She looked scared and confused.

"I'd like to go in by myself first," Riley said confidently.

"Are you sure?" Lieutenant Nico questioned. "We're not here for girls' time, you know. We're here to tell her about April and get out."

Riley shot him a stern look, slightly offended by his statement. "Yeah, I'm well aware, sir. Thank you. I just think easing her into the idea of her daughter still being alive after seven months is better than just springing it on her with no context. You didn't even tell her why she was here." Riley barked.

"Well, yeah, maybe you're right." He said, looking down at his notepad.

"I am right." Riley's chest flared proudly. "April, you're going to stay with Lieutenant Nico, and you're going to watch me and your…" She paused. "You're going to watch me through here, okay?" Riley smiled, pointing at the window.

"Okay!" April happily held her arms out to the lieutenant.

Once she was settled, Riley approached the door. She grabbed the handle and took a deep breath. After clicking it open, a rush of bright light hit her face.

She squinted her eyes to adjust, and when she did, she saw Amari's face beaming with a mixture of excitement and bewilderment. She stood up from her chair, unable to move closer because of the chains.

"RILEY?" She shouted. Riley closed the door behind her and ran to Amari. She hugged her over the table, and a loud bang radiated off the walls. It was the officer's way of telling her she wasn't allowed to make contact. They quickly broke their embrace and sat down.

"What is going on, teach? They brought me here, changed my clothes, and didn't tell me anything! I tried asking them questions, but nobody would budge! Why are you here? What's going on? I've been trying to call you for days now!" Panic trembled through her vocal cords. Riley lowered her eyes and smiled. Tears streamed down her face and onto the floor. Uncertainty now covered Amari's face.

"Please tell me what is going on before I lose my mind," Amari begged.

"I found her," Riley said calmly, wiping the tears from her eyes.

Amari's jaw dropped in disbelief. Tears welled in her eyes, too. "April...you found April? Well, where was she? It was that creep Quincy, wasn't it? See, I told you that guy was no good. I knew he had something to do with it..."

Amari rambled loudly, but Riley's ears filtered the noise into nothingness. She watched Amari's mouth move. Words continued to pour, but Riley heard absolute silence.

"This is going to be the best moment of my life," Riley said to herself. *"Tell her. TELL HER!"* Her brain repeated.

"Riley...are you okay?" Amari asked.

Riley snapped back. "Amari, I found her."

"Uh, yes, I know. You told me that, but where the hell has she been?" Amari asked, puzzled by the conversation.

"She's...she's been here. Here the whole time." Riley stumbled over her words.

"Riley, did they drug you? You're not making any sense." Amari waved her hand in front of Riley's face.

"Show her. Open the door." Her mind raced.

She turned around to motion Lieutenant Nico to bring in April. Grabbing both of Amari's hands, Riley looked deeply into her eyes.

"We have been looking for the same girl the entire time." She said softly, nearly whispering.

"What do you mean..." Amari asked concerningly, slowly pulling her hands away from Riley's.

The door to the interrogation room swung open, and out came Lieutenant Nico holding April...Lauren...in his arms. Riley looked at Amari, whose jaw was on the floor. Drool poured from the sides of her lips. Riley grabbed her wrists again and squeezed her hands tightly.

"Amari, I found her."

Amari let her head fall on the table and profusely sobbed into Riley's arms. She looked up slowly to stare into her daughter's beautiful green eyes. Lauren clung to Lieutenant Nico, unsure of why the stranger in front of her was so upset. Amari stood from her seat to get a better look while tears pooled on her shirt. Lauren started to whine with fear swirling in her eyes. She reached for Riley, who promptly grabbed her from Lieutenant Nico. Lauren looked at Amari concerningly, observing every teardrop that fell from her eyes.

Riley tapped Lauren on the shoulder. "This is all a little silly, huh? But this, this is your mommy. Your *real* mommy."

"Mama?" Lauren questioned, ping-ponging back and forth between Amari and Riley. Amari shook her head.

"Yes...yes, baby. Mama. I'm your mama! Don't you remember?" Amari's soothing voice seemed to do the trick, and Lauren returned to her normal, bubbly self.

"Would you like to give her a hug?" Riley asked Lauren. She promptly shook her head yes.

Riley handed Lauren to Amari, and she squeezed her tightly. She silently wept into her tie-dye shirt. Amari gently smelled her skin and gripped the back of her head, running her fingers through her bouncy curls. She began to belly-laugh uncontrollably like she was being tickled.

"Baby girl, what did they do to your hair?" She said, observing its dark black color with subtle blonde roots. "Did someone dye your precious blonde hair? How could they!"

Amari sat back down with Lauren in her lap, playing with her fingers and poking her belly to make her laugh. Their eyes never unlocked from each other's. She rested Lauren's head on her chest and continued to cry.

"I just don't understand. This is my Lauren…but also your April? What…what happened to her?"

"Kendra and Quincy happened," Riley said emotionlessly.

Amari's eyes widened as she gripped her daughter tightly.

"You would not believe the past 48 hours I've been through, but here are the cliff notes," Riley stated, counting on her fingers. "Kendra bailed me out seemingly as a last resort because she truly didn't know where April, really Lauren, was. Quincy admitted to Kendra kidnapping her, and also bringing her back to…Travis."

"TRAVIS?" Amari yelled with anger. "He had my baby this whole time? I KNEW IT, I JUST KNEW IT." She quickly settled back in her seat, trying her best not to scare Lauren. "Riley, I knew he had something to do with this. They made me seem like I was crazy and kept me locked up, but a mother's intuition is never wrong!" She passionately yelled, making direct eye contact with Lieutenant Nico in the corner of the room.

"Well, Travis didn't have anything to do with this until Quincy brought her to him," Riley said, slumping back in her seat.

"Well, I still knew he would be involved. Whatever, keep going." Amari scoffed.

"Kendra and Quincy knocked me out and tied me up. Kendra stormed off to Travis' house to take Lauren back by any means necessary. Quincy then forced me to go after her."

Amari sat speechless, egging Riley for more information as she rubbed Lauren's back.

"I got to Travis's house and..." Riley paused.

"And what? What happened? Was Travis there?" Amari asked.

"He's dead, Amari. Kendra killed him, thinking she could get to Lauren."

Amari gasped, covering her mouth with one hand and Lauren's ear with the other.

"Travis is...dead? He's dead!" Amari sulked.

"And I watched it happen."

"You were there? My god!"

"I was, and then I ran out the door with April-" Riley shook her head. "With Lauren in my arms, as fast as I could. We ran into the woods and stayed there until I could, uh, hook up with the police." Riley said, looking back at Lieutenant Nico standing in the corner. Playing coy, he smiled and waved to Amari. She scoffed again.

"Okay, so...Travis is dead. Quincy is...?"

"M.I.A. We think he got shot when he was trying to save me and Lauren, so we could escape."

"What the...what? I can't...I can't absorb all this right now."

"Nobody is asking you to. This is a lot to take in." Riley reached forward to grab her hands again. "The moral of the story is, your daughter is alive. She's safe. She's happy. And she is without a doubt the bit of light this screwed-up world needs right now." Amari sobbed again, wiping her tears with her sleeves.

"Time to wrap this up." Lieutenant Nico said, looking at his watch.

"Hold up there, buddy," Amari said bluntly. The lieutenant scowled from her superlative. "Sir, hold up there, sir. Where is she going to go? What's going to happen to her?" Panic was setting in once again.

"I'm taking her." Riley chimed in abruptly.

"You are?" Amari asked

"I will look after her until they let you out of here. That's a promise." A single tear streamed down her face.

"Actually, that won't be necessary, Ms. Michaels." Lieutenant Nico chimed in.

"What? What do you mean?"

"Remember that handshake we had back at my office? Well, the immunity didn't just cover you; it covered Ms. Syke as well." That sneaky smirk emerged on his face again.

Riley couldn't comprehend what she was hearing.

"You mean..."

"Yes, Ms. Syke is coming with us."

Amari's lips quivered, repeatedly thanking him. The lieutenant walked over to Amari and unlinked her chains from around her ankles. All three girls lunged into an embrace.

"I don't even know what to say. Because of you, my kid will never have to see me behind bars." Amari whispered in Riley's ear. The wetness from her eyes flowed onto Riley's cheeks.

"You don't have to say anything. We both found what we were looking for." Amari released her grip from Riley's back and kissed Lauren on the cheek.

Riley, Amari, and Lauren followed Lieutenant Nico out the door and into the hallway. He called over his shoulder as the girls trailed behind him. "So, where are we headed?"

Riley and Amari both looked at Lauren lovingly and in unison, calmly breathed.

"Home."